The New York Times

PUBLIC PROFILES

Cult Leaders

CHARLES MANSON, JIM JONES AND OTHERS

THE NEW YORK TIMES EDITORIAL STAFF

Published in 2020 by New York Times Educational Publishing
in association with The Rosen Publishing Group, Inc.
29 East 21st Street, New York, NY 10010

First Edition

The New York Times
Alex Ward: Editorial Director, Book Development
Phyllis Collazo: Photo Rights/Permissions Editor
Heidi Glovine: Administrative Manager

Rosen Publishing
Megan Kellerman: Managing Editor
Greg Tucker: Creative Director
Brian Garvey: Art Director

Cataloging-in-Publication Data
Names: New York Times Company.
Title: Cult leaders: Charles Manson, Jim Jones and others / edited by the New York Times editorial staff.
Description: New York : New York Times Educational Publishing, 2019. | Series: Public profiles | Includes glossary and index.
Identifiers: ISBN 9781642822427 (library bound) | ISBN 9781642822410 (pbk.) | ISBN 9781642822434 (ebook)
Subjects: LCSH: Cults—United States—Juvenile literature. | Religious biography—United States—Juvenile literature. | Cults—United States—History—Juvenile literature.
Classification: LCC BL2525.C858 2019 | DDC 291.9'0973—dc23

Manufactured in the United States of America

On the cover: Charles Manson, leader of the Manson family cult and accused mastermind in the killing of Sharon Tate and several others, arrives in court to enter a plea to seven counts of murder and one count of conspiracy; Bettmann/Getty Images.

Contents

CHAPTER 2

Jim Jones: The People's Temple

CHAPTER 3

David Koresh: The Branch Davidians

CHAPTER 5

Keith Raniere: Nxivm

Introduction

CULT LEADERS ARE powerful people. They attract followers by promising a new way of life. Maybe it's free love and subverting the establishment or a community founded on a unique political doctrine. It could be a path to the next life. Or perhaps it's a method for spiritual fulfillment or personal and professional success. To participate, followers are required to be completely subservient to their leader and to make enormous personal sacrifice. Once in a cult, it is extremely difficult to leave.

Cult leaders tend to be megalomaniacs. Described as charismatic, intense and magnetic, they are also narcissistic and totalitarian. They have a vision — sometimes clearly articulated, sometimes not — of the way life should be. And they manipulate others — the vulnerable, disenfranchised or lonely — into giving up everything else to become a part of it. Followers quit jobs and cut ties with family and friends. They donate their money and cars and houses to the group. They believe so completely in their leaders that they do whatever the leaders tell them to do — live in squalor, steal, submit to sexual slavery, punish themselves, kill others, slay their children and commit suicide.

The cult leaders selected for this book are among the most infamous, with extensive news coverage of the events surrounding the growth and demise of each of their cults. These leaders left deep impressions on the popular imagination. Charles Manson, whose Manson family murdered nine people in 1969 in an effort to start a revolution, became an underground legend. His songs and lyrics were recorded by rock bands, images of his face appeared on t-shirts and he and his followers were the subjects of books, movies and even a musical opera.

ANDREW COUNCILL FOR THE NEW YORK TIMES

Visitors enter beneath notorious faces of American crime, including Charles Manson, at the Museum of Crime and Punishment in Washington, D.C.

Jim Jones orchestrated the murder-suicides of more than 900 people in Jonestown, Guyana, in 1978. Under scrutiny for alleged human rights violations, Jones urged the entire population of the socialist town he founded to swallow a cyanide-laced grape drink mix in an act of political protest. They did, and the phrase "drinking the Kool-Aid" became a popular phrase for blind obedience.

The Texas city of Waco became famous after the annihilation of David Koresh and his Branch Davidians at a compound there in 1993. Armed with weapons and supplies, the group withstood a 51-day siege by the federal authorities. Seventy-nine people were consumed by a fire that started during an attempt to flush out Koresh. No one knows whether Koresh, who died from a gunshot wound to the head, committed suicide or was killed by a member of his devoted group.

In 1997, Heaven's Gate leader Marshall Applewhite convinced 38 followers to join him in a mass suicide so their souls could board an extraterrestrial spacecraft they believed followed the Hale-Bopp comet. The reclusive, tech-savvy group posted many of their leader's teachings on the Heaven's Gate website, which was used to recruit new members. Applewhite is dead, but the website is still live.

The Executive Success Program offered by Keith Raniere's self-help group Nxivm (pronounced Nex-e-um) appealed to people — mostly women — who could afford its expensive sessions. Each program led to another, indoctrinating attendees in Mr. Raniere's ideology. A select few women were invited to join a secret sisterhood within Nxivm, where they were branded and forced into what some described as sexual slavery. A series of news stories about the secret society resulted in Mr. Raniere's arrest in 2018, and Nxivm suspended operations shortly afterward.

The morbid fascination with cults and their leaders transcends mere curiosity. How could someone be talked into giving a near-stranger his life savings? Or sleeping with any man she is told to? Killing a child with cyanide? Taking his own life? Cult leaders are masters of manipulation. They know how to tap into the fears, hopes and desires of those looking for something different from the life they have. The fascination with cults stems from the fear that anyone could fall prey to the insatiable, egotistical, power-hungry drives of a cult leader.

CHAPTER 1

Charles Manson: The Manson Family

Once considered the most dangerous man alive, Charles Manson looked the part, with wild eyes and a swastika carved into his forehead. Manson had an intense charisma, and a talent for singing and songwriting. In his early 20s, he hoped to land a recording contract. When that failed to materialize, Manson began to travel around California, talking about the power of music, free love and the problem with the establishment. He attracted a group of young, disenfranchised followers. They called themselves the Manson family. And they murdered nine people.

3 Suspects in Tate Case Tied to Guru and 'Family'

BY STEVEN V. ROBERTS | DEC. 3, 1969

CHATSWORTH, CALIF., DEC. 2 — Here in the barren, boulder-strewn Santa Susanna Mountains, the persons accused of killing Sharon Tate, the actress, and at least seven other victims lived a life of indolence, free sex, midnight motorcycle races and apparently blind obedience to a mysterious guru.

This picture emerges from interviews with employees of the Spahn Ranch, a dilapidated riding stable whose Western-style buildings are sometimes used as a movie set.

It was here that Charles Manson and his "family" of about 18 young people lived for a number of months before the murder of Miss Tate

BETTMANN/GETTY IMAGES

Charles Manson, guru of the "family" whose members are held for the Tate murders.

and four others in a lonely hillside home on Aug. 9. They left about a week after the killings when policemen raided their camp looking for stolen automobiles and made several arrests.

Manson, 34 years old, has not been charged in the murder case but three other members of the "family" have. Manson is being held in Independence, Calif., on charges of suspicion of arson and receiving stolen goods.

The third suspect in the murder case was arrested in Concord, N.H., today. She is Linda Louise Kasabian, 19, cited on five counts of murder. Two other suspects in custody are Charles D. Watson, 23, held in McKinney, Tex., and Patricia Krenwinkel, 21, held in Mobile, Ala.

Six other persons are believed held in Los Angeles in connection with the murders, but the police would not discuss their relationship with the case.

Today, persons who knew Manson were afraid to talk about him publicly. "He's got his zombies out," said one employee of the Spahn ranch. "There's more than one family that's been conditioned to believe that Charlie Manson is always right."

Manson and the "family" were allowed to stay on the Spahn ranch simply because people were afraid of him.

"I couldn't get rid of them," said George Spahn, the elderly, blind owner of the ranch, sitting in a fly-covered room with dogs and saddles scattered everywhere.

"I smelled a rat but I was afraid to crowd them. I was scared to death of Charlie. I was afraid that if I crossed him he'd hurt me. I guess I got it right."

The next home for the nomadic band was a ranch near Death Valley, where they set up a fortress-like camp guarded by sentries and reportedly continued their car-stealing activities. They remained there until mid-October when policemen moved in and arrested Manson and several others on charges of receiving stolen property.

The "family" — about six men and 12 women — arrived in a broken-down school bus after a slow trip from San Francisco's Haight-Ashbury district. During cold spells they slept in the abandoned buildings of the movie set but during the summer they camped out in the fields and woods.

Those who knew the group say they slept late and often stayed up most of the night, racing motorcycles on Santa Susanna Pass Road or singing. During the day they walked in the mountains or went on "garbage trips" to collect unwanted food from local merchants. They bought gas with a credit card one girl had stolen from her parents.

"They lived very carelessly," said one man who knew them. "It was a real monotonous life but they kept telling themselves they were happy."

The center of this life was Manson, who has a five-page police record stretching back 18 years. Little is known of his early life, but several years ago he started collecting young girls with a powerful magnetic attraction.

The lawyer for one of his followers, Susan Denise Atkins, said today that his client was under "hypnotic spells" from Manson. Another girl, Sandra Pugh, told a reporter:

"He was magnetic. His motions were like magic, it seemed like. The first time I saw him he was petting a cat. I don't know why that struck me, but he seemed so kind."

The girls living with Manson told people that they loved him, that they had been thrown out by their parents, that they had nowhere else to go.

"He played the guitar, he sang, he would make love to a girl," said one employee of the Spahn ranch. "He preached love and peace and all that, you know. He conditioned the girls to do anything."

Head of 'Family' Is Held for Trial

BY STEVEN V. ROBERTS | DEC. 4, 1969

LOS ANGELES, DEC. 3 — Charles Manson, the guru nomad whose followers have been sought for at least eight murders in the Los Angeles area, was bound over today to Superior Court in Independence, Calif., following a pretrial hearing. He faces charges of receiving stolen property and auto theft.

Manson was ordered to stand trial on the charges in Superior Court. Bond was put at $25,000 and he was returned to jail. An arraignment was scheduled for Dec. 12.

Manson and several dozen followers were arrested in mid-October when the police raided their fortified encampment near Death Valley. He had been held in Independence as a Federal parole violator while awaiting disposition of the theft charges.

Three members of Manson's so-called "family" of wandering youths have been arrested for the murder Aug. 9 of Sharon Tate, the actress, and four other victims. Members of the "family" have also been linked to the slaying of a musician and two owners of a grocery chain.

MORE WARRANTS DUE

One of the three "family" members, Linda Louise Kasabian, 20 years old, waived extradition and flew to Los Angeles tonight from New Hampshire, where she had surrendered to the police yesterday. The two other murder suspects will probably fight extradition. They are Charles Watson, 24, now in prison in McKinney, Tex., and Patricia Krenwinkel, 21, who is in custody in Mobile, Ala.

The police say they will probably issue four or five more murder warrants in the case, which goes before a Los Angeles County grand jury Friday.

In addition to Manson, who is 35, four youths are being held in Independence on charges stemming from the October raid. Manson has a police record going back 18 years. He has apparently been able to attract an extremely loyal following of young people, particularly girls, who consider themselves his "slaves" and refer to him as "god" and "satan."

In addition to Miss Tate, those slain at her home in Santa Monica on the morning of Aug. 9 were Jay Sebring, Wojciech Frykowski, Abigail Folger and Steven Parent.

As outlined to the Los Angeles grand jury, the killers purportedly went to the house because Terry Melcher, son of Doris Day, the actress, once lived there and reportedly had promised the leader of a hippie cult a recording date, which was never fulfilled. The leader directed his followers to kill everyone at the house as a symbol of rejection. But the leader did not go to the house.

Charlie Manson, Nomadic Guru, Flirted With Crime in a Turbulent Childhood

BY STEVEN V. ROBERTS | DEC. 7, 1969

LOS ANGELES, DEC. 6 — "Charlie pulled me up one day out in the desert," Juan Flynn said the other day, recalling a recent conversation with Charles Manson. "There were tears in his eyes and he said: 'Juan, when they catch me, it's going to be like feeding me to the lions. They're going to put me far away because I have no family, no one that will help me.

" 'When I was in jail,' " Juan continued, quoting his friend, 'I noticed the bulls [guards] in there used to keep track of everything — the letters you got, the visitors who remembered you in there. I knew they could do anything to me, because I had nobody.' "

Not long after that conversation, Charles Manson was caught. The police raided a hideout near Death Valley, where he lived with several dozen youthful followers, and arrested them for stealing automobiles and receiving stolen property.

That was in mid-October. Last Monday, the Los Angeles police issued warrants for the arrest of three people, one man and two women, who had belonged to Manson's "family" of wanderers. They were charged with the murder of Sharon Tate, the actress, and four others last Aug. 9, and were under suspicion for at least six other killings in the Los Angeles area.

SLAVISH DEVOTION

On Friday, the Los Angeles District Attorney asked a grand jury to indict Manson, who was still in jail on changes stemming from the Death Valley raid, and six of his friends for the Tate murders. Indictments were also requested in the slaying of Leno and Rosemary

LaBianca, owners of a grocery chain, who were killed the night after Miss Tate was found dead.

Manson is a slight man, about 5 feet 7 inches tall, with dark, shoulder-length hair. For the last two years, he has lived at the center of a band of young drifters, mainly girls, who follow his whims and wishes with almost slavish devotion.

The trail that led Charles Manson to California and to the "family" he never had before is one that includes a searing childhood and a crime-ridden youth. His story, patched together from interviews with acquaintances and the public records he has left behind, is a turbulent one.

Manson was born into loneliness. His mother was a teenager in Cincinnati when she became pregnant by one of her many boyfriends, reportedly an Army colonel. Wanting to give her child a name, she married William Manson shortly before her son was born on Nov. 11, 1934.

The boy never knew the colonel or Mr. Manson. His mother moved and the boy was sent to live with his grandmother and a maternal aunt in West Virginia. The aunt was a harsh disciplinarian, he recalled later, and punished him severely when he left his yard to play with other children.

When Manson was 13, his uncle fell ill with tuberculosis and the youngster rejoined his mother in Indianapolis. The woman did not want him and tried to get him placed in a foster home. He had previously lived in several foster homes, including one on a farm, and once told the juvenile authorities that his dream in life was to become a farmer.

RUNNING AWAY

When the foster home could not be arranged, his mother sent Manson to the Gibault School in Terre Haute, Ind., a boarding school run by Roman Catholic priests. When his mother could not keep up the payments at Gibault, Manson returned home, but quickly ran away. His mother was frequently drunk, he said, and living with a succession of men. “I didn’t want to stay where mother lived in sin,” he told juvenile officials in Indianapolis.

At the age of 14, he rented a room and supported himself by delivering messages for Western Union and by petty theft. The robbery of $9 from a grocery store put him back in the hands of the juvenile authorities. He did not want to go home, he said. Soon it was a moot question; his mother left town after getting arrested for adultery.

About this time, young Manson came under the attention of the Rev. George Powers, a local priest. “This particular boy seemed very lonesome, just craving attention and affection,” recalled Father Powers, now an instructor at the New York Theological Seminary. “He looked like an innocent altar boy, and he was so ashamed of his mother.”

Father Powers arranged for Manson to be sent to Boys Town near Omaha, and the Indianapolis newspaper ran a big story. “He won everybody over,” the priest said. “The juvenile court judge was completely taken with his personality. He had an ability beyond his years to present himself; he was a beautiful kid for his age.”

BACK TO INDIANA

Manson arrived in Boys Town in March of 1949. Four days later, he ran away and stole a motor scooter, then a car. He was arrested, while robbing a grocery store, in Peoria, Ill., and sent back to Indianapolis. Officials there, puzzled and frustrated, sent him to reform school in Plainfield, Ind.

For the next five years, Manson was in and out of institutions. In 1954, he returned to West Virginia where his grandmother and aunt lived, and married Rosalie Jean Willis on Jan. 17, 1955. Some reports indicate that they had a son, and, that by the time the child was born, Manson was in jail in California for transporting stolen vehicles.

When he was released in September 1958, his wife had already divorced him. He was arrested several times for theft, forgery and probation violations. In 1960, he was arrested for violating the White

Slave Traffic Act in Laredo, Tex., and when he was returned to Los Angeles, he was sentenced to 10 years in jail for check forgery and probation violations.

During his stay at McNeil Island Penitentiary in Washington state, Manson took up new interests: Music, philosophy, and Scientology, a pseudoreligious cult then becoming popular on the West Coast.

Charles Manson started a new life after his release on March 21, 1967. He headed for the Haight-Ashbury district of San Francisco, where the hippie movements was centered. Soon he started exercising what appeared to be enormous power over women and his clan began to grow.

PART OF HIS GROUP

"Charlie always had first crack at the new girl," a male friend recalled recently. "But he also used them as bait. He'd share them with you, but if you accepted you were part of his group, you were obligated to him."

About a year later Manson and his "family" piled into an old school bus and headed south for Los Angeles. His interest in music had grown and he had made friends with various musical figures: Gary Hinman, a musician who let the group stay in his home at Malibu (where he was found murdered last July); Dennis Wilson of the Beach Boys, a popular singing group and Terry Melcher, a young producer who lived in the home near Beverly Hills in which Sharon Tate was later murdered.

The group stayed in various borrowed accommodations for a while and then settled at the Spahn Ranch, an old western movie set and riding stable in the Santa Susanna Mountains about 20 miles northwest of downtown Los Angeles.

The ranch's owner was not overjoyed about the arrangement, but he was too old and blind and frightened to object. He even helped the group out with its grocery bills — and installed an alarm system in his bedroom.

'ALL THERE IS, MAN'

While the membership of the "family" shifted constantly, it generally consisted of about 12 girls and six boys living an indolent life of easy sex (several girls had babies that members of the family delivered themselves), plentiful marijuana (but few hard drugs), and such projects as converting the "Longhorn Saloon" on the movie set into communal sleeping quarters.

What attracted people to Manson's family? He found lonely outcasts like himself, and they gave each other the affection' they had always sought and seldom found. "That's all there is, man," Manson often told friends. "If you don't have someone to love you, you don't have anything."

Attorneys for several of the defendants in the Tate murders contend that Manson had a "hypnotic effect" on his followers, but his friends tend to scoff at the theory. "It's not hypnotism," said one, "it's making good love to the girls."

"He gave off a lot of magic," said one of his girls. "Everyone was always so happy around him." Another said: "He's got the look that he needs to be mothered."

Manson's followers tended to be young and "impressionable" girls, said one acquaintance. Often they had trouble at home with their parents. Several had early and unhappy marriages.

AN ECLECTIC PHILOSOPHY

"You're brought up to believe that you can't have sex unless you're married," explained one girl who was close to the family. "Here girls could do whatever they wanted, they didn't have to worry about getting caught or toeing the mark. Charlie always said 'you don't have to answer to anybody, you can be whatever you want to be.' "

The precept of individuality was at the basis of an eclectic philosophy that Manson preached to his followers. "He used to say all the time, 'each man is a god, I am god, and you are god,' " one friend recalled.

At the same time Manson could explode with fury at people who disagreed with him. When a neighbor complained about motorcycle racing late at night, a hand at the Spahn Ranch said, Manson told him: "Shut up, you son of a bitch, or I'll burn your goddamn house down." Friends called him "Hymie" behind his back, by which they meant "Hitler."

His anger was usually directed at those he considered comfortable and successful. He said "society" was "corrupting" the minds of children and not letting them think for themselves. He hated the term "hippie," because he felt the "establishment" used it as an equivalent of "nigger."

He admired the Beatles. He sent them singing telegrams and found deep meaning in some of their songs. One of his favorites, called "Piggies," has this verse:

Everywhere there's lots of piggies
Living piggy lives
You can see them out for dinner
With their piggy wives
Clutching forks and knives to eat their bacon

Friends said Manson desperately wanted to make his own record as a way of reaching the public and resented several friends who failed to help him get a recording contract.

He had a deep fear of the black power movement. It was Manson's conviction, friends said, that militant blacks would soon "take over" the country, and he was apparently fortifying his desert encampment to fend them off. The group had a number of guns and often practiced with them at the Spahn Ranch.

The girls were sewing clothes that they said would be particularly durable for the siege in the desert.

"I always thought good and evil were fighting for control of Charlie," a longtime friend said recently. "He could be the most charming person alive and then something would touch him off. I guess the evil finally won out."

Manson Called a Megalomaniac by Prosecutor as Trial Begins

BY DOUGLAS ROBINSON | JULY 25, 1970

LOS ANGELES, JULY 24 — Charles M. Manson, the hippie cult leader accused of planning and ordering the murder of seven persons in the Los Angeles area last year, was described in court today as a "megalomaniac who coupled his insatiable thirst for power with an intense obsession for violent death."

The description came in the opening statement of Deputy District Attorney Vincent T. Bugliosi. The statement marked the official opening of the trial of Manson and three young women followers for the murders of Sharon Tate, the actress, and six other persons.

Manson himself appeared the courtroom with an X slashed in his forehead, a wound apparently caused by a razor blade. A statement from the defendant, distributed by his attorney, explained that the self-mutilation represented society's rejection of Manson as a man.

"I am considered inadequate and incompetent to speak or defend myself in your court," the statement read. "You have created the monster. I am not of you, from you, nor do condone your wars or your unjust attitudes towards things, animals and people that you won't try to understand. I have Xed myself from your world."

QUESTIONS FOR THE JURY

In his opening statement, Mr. Bugliosi, the deputy district attorney, said the state would attempt to prove that Manson was a "vagrant wanderer, a frustrated singer and guitarist, a pseudo-philosopher, but, most of all, a killer who cleverly masqueraded behind the common image of a hippie, that of being peace-loving."

"What kind of diabolical, satanic mind would contemplate or conceive of these mass murders?" Mr. Bugliosi asks the jury of seven men and five women. "What kind of mind would want to have seven human beings brutally murdered?"

"We expect the evidence at his trial to show Charles Manson owned that diabolical mind," the prosecutor continued. "Charles Manson, who the evidence will show at times has had the infinite humility to call himself Jesus Christ."

Mr. Bugliosi also suggested several motives for the killings, including an "obsession" with the possibility of a revolution between blacks and whites, which he called "Helter Skelter," the title of a song recorded by the Beatles.

Manson, the prosecutor said, was an avid follower of the Beatles and "believed that they were speaking to him through the lyrics of their songs."

To Manson, Mr. Bugliosi continued, "Helter Skelter" meant the black man's rising up against the white establishment and murdering the entire white race, with the exception of Manson and his chosen followers, who intended to escape from Helter Skelter by going to the desert.

The words "Helter Skelter" were scrawled in blood at the scene of the murder of Mr. and Mrs. Leno LaBianca of Los Angeles, who were stabbed to death the night after the Tate murders.

Manson and his three co-defendants, Patricia Krenwinkel, Susan Denise Atkins and Leslie Van Houten, are accused of planning and carrying out the LaBianca murders. But Miss Houten did not participate in the Tate killings, the prosecution says, as did the others, according to the state.

Another person accused of the crimes, Charles D. Watson, is in custody in Texas. He has been successful in delaying his extradition to California to stand trial.

In his opening remarks, Mr. Bugliosi suggested that the scrawling of the word "pig" at the scene of the murders was an attempt by Manson to make it look as though the killings had been carried out by blacks. This, in turn, would spark the revolution, he said.

MORE OF AN ARGUMENT

"Manson envisioned the black people, once they destroyed the white race and assumed the reins of power," the prosecutor said, "[as being] unable to, handle the reins of power because of inexperience." They would have to "turn them over to those white people who had escaped from Helter Skelter," he said.

"This, of course, means Manson and his followers," he said. "In Manson's mind, his family, and particularly he, would be the ultimate beneficiaries of the black-white civil war."

Mr. Bugliosi's opening statement was repeatedly interrupted by Irving A. Kanarek, Manson's attorney, who contended that the speech was more of an argument than an opening statement.

During the rest of the opening court session, the jury heard testimony from several parents of the victims and from Mrs. Winifred Chapman, the housekeeper at the Tate home who discovered the five bodies Aug. 9.

Mrs. Linda Kasabian, another defendant in the murders, is expected to testify for the state on Monday. Mrs. Kasabian, who allegedly drove the killers to the scene of the crimes, will be offered immunity from prosecution for her testimony.

Manson: The Two Faces of a Man on Trial

BY STEVEN V. ROBERTS | JAN. 3, 1971

LOS ANGELES — Charles Manson has probably been on as many magazines covers in the last year as anyone — a lofty achievement for the son of a teen-age prostitute. This strange little man, now standing trial here for seven murders, has come to symbolize a basic conflict in a society that often seems at war with its own young.

As the six-month trial of Manson and three female followers moved slowly toward its conclusion last week, the closing arguments on both sides focused on the tribal leader and what he represented. Prosecutor Vincent Bugliosi called him a man with a "crazed, frenzied" mind who espoused "bizarre, weird concepts.... He's nothing but a cold-blooded murderer who places absolutely no value on another human being's life."

'SCROUNGY NOBODY'

Several weeks before, Manson had taken the stand in his own behalf, and in a remarkable, rambling discourse had sketched a different picture. He was a "little old scroungy nobody" whose "father" had been the prisons in which he spent most of his youth, Manson said. "I was given a name and a number and I was put in a cell and I have lived in a cell with a name and a number... . I don't know who I am. I am whatever you make me, but what you want is a fiend. You want a sadistic fiend because that is what you are."

For three days Mr. Bugliosi recounted the now familiar charges — that Manson had ordered four members of his nomadic band to go to an isolated, hilltop house, where he had once been a visitor, and kill the occupants. The main motive, the prosecutor said, was to create "helter skelter," a phrase taken from a song by the Beatles, which to Manson meant a race war between blacks and whites. Manson often wore the mask of a "peace-loving guy," Mr. Bugliosi concluded, but he really harbored "an insatiable lust for death, blood and murder."

Paul Fitzgerald, who often acts as chief defense counsel, replied that Manson and his co-defendants — the prosecution called them "mindless robots" — were being tried for breaking many of the Ten Commandments, not just the Fifth. Their real crime, in the eyes of society, was their lifestyle. They should not be convicted, the lawyer argued, for "running away from home, eating garbage, making love, being different, living in the desert, loving Charles Manson, hating others or preaching a radical philosophy."

The cleavage between the defendants and most middle-class Americans, including the jury, was illustrated when Irving Kanarek, another defense lawyer, mentioned that during the period of the murders, Manson had been occupied with a new girlfriend. "He was sleeping with her more or less continually," said Mr. Kanarek, who then hastily assured the jury that he did not share his client's morals and that he did not think they did, either.

Any visitor to the courthouse here can catch a glimpse of the Manson "family" lifestyle. About a dozen members gather in and around the courtroom almost every day. And three of them have taken up permanent residence in a dilapidated van parked outside the building. They look like almost any group of teenagers with their faded jeans and occasional pimples, except for the "X" some of them have seared into their foreheads as a sign of loyalty to Manson and the "family." They are obviously devoted to the guru, but they also stay together, as one girl put it, because "we have nowhere else to go."

These are the wanderers, the rejects, hitching a ride from Nowhere to Oblivion, looking for a place to belong. "These children that come at you with knives, they are your children," Manson told the court. "You taught them. I didn't teach them. I just tried to help them stand up.

"Most of the people at the ranch that you call the 'family' were just people that were alongside the road, that their parents had kicked them out or they did not want to go to Juvenile Hall. So I did the best I could and I took them up to my garbage dump. I told them this: that in love there is no wrong."

These are the two faces of Charles Manson — the cold-blooded killer and the neglected waif. Most observers at the trial believe both may be accurate that the little man who preached love for all men may well have been responsible for the death of at least seven of them.

Manson Case: People Keep Asking — 'What Made Those Kids Do It?'

OPINION | BY STEVEN V. ROBERTS | JAN. 31, 1971

LOS ANGELES — During his closing arguments in the Sharon Tate murder trial, prosecutor Vincent Bugliosi described Charles Manson as a "man of a thousand faces," each catering to the different needs and expectations of his companions. Indeed, Manson was so sensitive to people, so sharp in picking the right face, that many of the girls he recruited for his nomadic band thought he was psychic.

Manson, however, described himself as a mirror, reflecting back to people images of themselves, images they wanted to see — or were afraid to see.

Last week, Manson and three of his female followers were convicted of a total of 27 counts of murder and conspiracy in the deaths of Miss Tate and six others in the summer of 1969. As the seven-month trial finally ended, it seemed that both Mr. Bugliosi and Manson were right. The defendant did have many faces — demon, hero, child, father, lover, waif. But he was also a mirror, reflecting pictures to a mesmerized public which then erected them into symbols of admiration and fear.

To some of the radical young he became a hero of the revolution, a man who had actually "offed the pigs." To the nation east of the Sierras, he seemed to symbolize the craziness of California, the weirdo capital of the country. To many average, middle-class people, Manson focused their fright, and their fascination with the younger generation; they saw him and his "family" as the vanguard of sinister forces that were turning the world on its head — or the heads on the world.

The trial verdicts were hardly a surprise. Most observers felt that even though the prosecution had not presented an airtight case, the evidence against the defendants was overwhelming. The defense did not even call any witnesses to rebut the prosecution.

Late in the week, the court began the penalty phase of the trial, which could take several weeks of testimony. Then the jury will decide whether to give the four defendants life imprisonment or the death sentence.

The imminent end of the trial, however, does not mean the end of Charlie Manson and his family. Few stories in recent years have so captured the public's attention. The strange guru and his girls are now part of the culture, and they call up a whole package of ideas and emotions.

• Among the counterculture, Manson achieved almost instant star status. He became the cover boy of the underground press, one of "us" merely because he was not one of "them."

Manson's popularity on the left paled a bit when it became clear that his political views were at best undeveloped, and at worst, absurd. He also fell victim to the growing feeling that random violence is counterproductive "adventurism." Nevertheless, long articles by and about him still appear in the underground press.

• Being from California in the Age of Manson has been rather unnerving, especially if your hair exceeds military length. The "hippie cult" as the headline writers liked to call it, seemed to confirm all the worst suspicions and stereotypes about Smogville-on-the-Pacific.

California, many in rest of the nation seemed convinced, was riven by some psychic San Andreas Fault that was about to crack wide open. One example: A movie company went to a small town in Texas to shoot a film and was greeted with considerable skepticism by the local citizenry. The reason, explained one gas station attendant, was that the movie people came from where "all them murders" took place.

• Manson and his family are most interesting, perhaps, as a symbol of youth in its most grotesque form, the ultimate end of all that dope and free sex and permissiveness, Spiro Agnew's worst nightmare. Most reporters covering the story found themselves constantly besieged with letters and questions. People were fascinated by the horror, like a parade of motorists slowing down to see a bad car wreck.

What people usually wanted to know was, "What made those kids do it?" And lurking behind that question was another, summed up in the magazine article that asked boldly, "Are your kids capable of murder?" No answer was ever really satisfactory. It couldn't happen, but then there were all those bodies…

Of course, the young people epitomized by the Manson family are part of a broader fear, a fear that things are out of control, that all the old assumptions and values don't count anymore. Yeats said, "The center cannot hold." To many people, Charles Manson is saying, "The center isn't there anymore."

STEVEN V. ROBERTS is a journalist at The New York Times.

How Charles Manson Nearly Made It in Hollywood

BY ALEX WILLIAMS | NOV. 21, 2017

FOR A FLEETING MOMENT in the confused swirl of the 1960s, Charles Manson, a diminutive ex-convict who had taken to hippie silks and a cosmic patter, somehow wormed his way into a plum spot adjacent the Hollywood A-list. He jammed with Neil Young, bunked with a Beach Boy and mingled with Mama Cass and Michael Caine at industry parties.

Before his Los Angeles experience turned very, very, very sour, Mr. Manson managed to pass himself off as enough of an insider to merit a thumbs up from Mr. Young. "This guy, you know, he's good," Mr. Young once told a Reprise record executive, in the days before the era-shattering murder spree. "He's just a little out of control."

The basic outline of Mr. Manson as a failed songwriter is familiar to anyone who has ever watched one of the dozens (hundreds?) of cable documentaries on the Manson family, or donned a Guns N' Roses concert T-shirt (the band covered Mr. Manson's "Look at Your Game, Girl" on its 1993 album, "The Spaghetti Incident?").

But he came closer to success than one might expect.

After a lengthy musical apprenticeship plucking his acoustic guitar in a cell, Mr. Manson, a self-described member of the Bing Crosby generation, was released from prison in 1967, just in time for the psychedelic explosion. After a stop in San Francisco's Haight Ashbury for a hippie makeover, he headed with a few members of his budding so-called family to Los Angeles to find fame and fortune as the next Dylan, or at least the next really creepy Dylan.

In classic Los Angeles fashion, his big break — or what looked like it — came through a chance encounter with a celebrity. After Dennis Wilson, the hard-partying drummer for the Beach Boys, picked up a couple of Mr. Manson's young female followers while hitchhiking, Mr.

ASSOCIATED PRESS

Charles Manson in Los Angeles in 1971.

Manson did his best to bring Mr. Wilson, with his sports cars and gold records, under his messianic spell.

The drummer was open to mind expansion, having studied under the Maharishi Mahesh Yogi. As Mr. Wilson explained to Britain's Record Mirror in 1968, he had met a new guru named Charlie, "who'd recently come out of jail after 12 years," but had "great musical ideas."

"We're writing together now," he said of the man he called the Wizard. "He's dumb, in some ways, but I accept his approach and have learnt from him."

Mr. Manson and his family camped out at Mr. Wilson's Pacific Palisades estate, once the home of Will Rogers. They mingled in the Beach Boys recording studio with the likes of Rodney Bingenheimer, the columnist and social arbiter of the Los Angeles rock scene who was eventually celebrated in the 2004 documentary "Mayor of the Sunset Strip."

Mr. Manson was also trying out his mystical psychobabble on every rock star he met. Not all were smitten.

One night, Mr. Wilson invited his cousin Mike Love, the Beach Boys singer, over for dinner to meet the Wizard. It quickly turned into a "group sex kind of situation," Mr. Love told ABC News many years later. "It wasn't my cup of tea, so I excused myself to take a shower."

"No sooner than I got in the shower, the door opened and Charlie Manson stood there and looked up at me and said, 'You can't do that,' " Mr. Love recalled. "I said, 'Excuse me?' " Mr. Manson apparently replied: "You can't leave the group!"

Despite Mr. Manson's unsettling behavior, the Beach Boys gave him his first taste of mainstream fame, including "Never Learn Not to Love," an only slightly reworked version of the Manson necro-rocker "Cease to Exist," on their 1969 album, "20/20." With lyrics like "Cease to resist, come on say you love me," it wasn't exactly a surfin' safari. Nevertheless, the band apparently thought enough of their Manson-inspired new direction to perform the song on "The Mike Douglas Show."

Mr. Manson also managed to win over Neil Young, who was already attaining legend status in Los Angeles at that time. In his 2012 autobiography, "Waging Heavy Peace," Mr. Young recalled a visit to his house by Mr. Manson and a few of the women, when Mr. Manson grabbed Mr. Young's guitar and started strumming a few originals.

"His songs were off-the-cuff things he made up as he went along," Mr. Young writes, "and they were never the same twice in a row. Kind of like Dylan, but different because it was hard to glimpse a true message in them, but the songs were fascinating. He was quite good."

It wasn't long before Mr. Manson was finding doors open for him at the most exclusive Hollywood parties. In his 1992 autobiography, "What's It All About?," Michael Caine, no hippie to be sure, recalled being introduced to a "scruffy little man" named Charles Manson at a party at Cass Elliot's house. (Also in attendance: future Manson family victims Sharon Tate and Jay Sebring, the celebrity hairstylist).

Not so different from the world today, an open-door policy was common in the late '60s, particularly for colorfully dressed hipsters carrying acoustic guitars and drugs.

More than a few Hollywood players explored free love with members of the Manson family, perhaps even with Mr. Manson himself. According to "Manson In His Own Words," a 1986 as-told-to book by Nuel Emmons, an old prison acquaintance, executives at a major record label supposedly were hooked when Mr. Manson started talking about his carefree existence "living in a bus with 12 girls."

Based on six years of interviews with a convicted murderer given to wild hyperbole and self-contradiction (many reconstructed without the benefit of a tape recorder), some of the subject's "recollections" need to be taken with a grain of salt, if not a pound of it. Nevertheless, Mr. Manson supposedly told Mr. Emmons that before long, he and his "girls" were on the "let's-get-acquainted list of many of the not-so-straight idols of the movie world."

"We had long ago chucked our inhibitions about sex," Mr. Manson supposedly said. "But chains, whips, torture and other weirdness were not part of our routine." The book also recounts a supposed ménage à trois with Mr. Manson, a male movie star and his television actress wife, after which the man, one "Mr. B," "slipped five one-hundred-dollar bills in my pocket."

Other members of the Hollywood firmament with actual names fell under his spell. In a 2014 interview with Britain's Daily Mail, Angela Lansbury talked about how her daughter, Deirdre, who had struggled with drug addiction as a teenager in the '60s, "was in with a crowd led by Charles Manson."

"She was one of many youngsters who knew him, and they were fascinated," Ms. Lansbury said. "He was an extraordinary character, charismatic in many ways, no question about it."

All tales of Mr. Manson's days living the Hollywood high life lead to Terry Melcher, the son of Doris Day who was a heavyweight record producer for acts including the Beach Boys and the Byrds. Along with Mr. Wilson and Gregg Jakobson, an industry friend, Mr. Melcher, who died in 2004, was "part of an informal society known as the Golden Penetrators," according to Jeff Guinn's exhaustive 2013 biography, "Manson: The Life and Times of Charles Manson."

The group's membership "was limited to anyone who had sex with women from one of show business's most famous families," but did not apparently stop there.

The "triumvirate reveled in their hedonism," Mr. Guinn writes. "In a city that had long ago waived most moral or legal limits for the famous, their philosophy was 'We're us, there are no rules, we get to do this.' "

Little surprise, then, that they were soon hanging out in a celebrity booth at the Whiskey a Go Go, with one Charles Milles Manson, who one night managed to clear the dance floor with his maniacal gyrations: "He tipped back his head and threw out his arms," Mr. Guinn writes. "It seemed as though electrical sparks flew from Charlie's fingers and hair."

"The crowd had surged off the dance floor as if driven by some irresistible force field," the book continues. "Now it circled the floor, mesmerized by the sight of the whirling dervish."

While Mr. Melcher was one of the music industry's power players, he was also known in the late '60s as one half of a celebrity couple, living with his girlfriend, Candice Bergen, in a secluded Benedict Canyon home at 10050 Cielo Drive.

Students of the period do not need to be told how things unfolded after Mr. Melcher met Mr. Manson. The producer initially showed interest in Mr. Manson's music, but eventually distanced himself.

And as Mr. Manson watched his chance at musical fame evaporate, he grew increasingly desperate and began to sermonize with more fervor about a coming race war that he called Helter Skelter, a phrase he cribbed from the Beatles song about an amusement-park ride.

For decades, debate has raged about the motives of the so-called Tate murders, even among those involved in them. It seems clear that, at some level, Mr. Manson sought to strike back at the Hollywood elite that had spurned him.

Regardless, Mr. Manson was well aware that Mr. Melcher no longer lived in the Cielo Drive house where five adults and Ms. Tate's unborn son died gruesomely. It was a house Mr. Manson knew well, and on the evening of March 23, 1969, fewer than five months before the murders, Mr. Manson had dropped by looking for Mr. Melcher, according to "Helter Skelter," the 1974 book by the Manson prosecutor Vincent Bugliosi, with Gary Gentry.

He found new residents in the house, however, who directed him to Rudi Altobelli, a talent manager who owned the house, but who was then staying in the guesthouse. Mr. Altobelli informed Mr. Manson that Mr. Melcher had moved to Malibu, but offered no address.

Mr. Manson's visit that day, it seems, would be the most fateful of his celebrity encounters. The next day, Ms. Tate mentioned the curious encounter to Mr. Altobelli on a flight to Rome. "Did you see that creepy-looking guy come back there yesterday?" she asked.

Charles Manson Dies at 83; Wild-Eyed Leader of a Murderous Crew

OBITUARY | BY MARGALIT FOX | NOV. 20, 2017

CHARLES MANSON, one of the most notorious murderers of the 20th century, who was very likely the most culturally persistent and perhaps also the most inscrutable, died on Sunday in a hospital in Kern County, Calif., north of Los Angeles. He was 83 and had been behind bars for most of his life.

The California Department of Corrections and Rehabilitation announced his death in a news release. In accordance with federal and state privacy regulations, no cause was given; he had been hospitalized in January for intestinal bleeding but was ruled too frail to undergo surgery.

Mr. Manson was a semiliterate habitual criminal and failed musician before he came to irrevocable attention in the late 1960s as the wild-eyed leader of the Manson family, a murderous band of young drifters in California. Convicted of nine murders in all, he was known in particular for the seven brutal killings collectively called the Tate-LaBianca murders, committed by his followers on two consecutive August nights in 1969.

The most famous of the victims was Sharon Tate, an actress who was married to the film director Roman Polanski. Eight and a half months pregnant, she was killed with four other people at her home in the Benedict Canyon area of Los Angeles, near Beverly Hills.

The Tate-LaBianca killings and the seven-month trial that followed were the subjects of fevered news coverage. To a frightened, mesmerized public, the murders, with their undercurrents of sex, drugs, rock 'n' roll and Satanism, seemed the depraved logical extension of the anti-establishment, do-your-own-thing ethos that helped define the '60s.

MEL MELCON/LOS ANGELES TIMES/GETTY IMAGES

Charles Manson was a constant dark presence in pop culture for decades after his arrest in the gruesome Tate-LaBianca murders.

Since then, the Manson family has occupied a dark, persistent place in American culture — and American commerce. It has inspired, among other things, pop songs, an opera, films, a host of internet fan sites, T-shirts, children's wear and half the stage name of the rock musician Marilyn Manson.

It has also been the subject of many nonfiction books, most famously "Helter Skelter" (1974), by Vincent Bugliosi and Curt Gentry. Mr. Bugliosi was the lead prosecutor at the Tate-LaBianca trial.

The Manson family came to renewed attention in 2008, when officials in California, responding to long speculation that there were victims still unaccounted for, searched a stretch of desert in Death Valley. There, in a derelict place known as the Barker Ranch, Mr. Manson and his followers had lived for a time in the late '60s. The search turned up no human remains.

ASSOCIATED PRESS

The five victims slain the night of Aug. 9, 1969, at the Benedict Canyon Estate of Roman Polanski. From left, Voityck Frykowski, Sharon Tate, Stephen Parent, Jay Sebring and Abigail Folger.

It was a measure of Mr. Manson's hold over his followers, mostly young women who had fled middle-class homes, that he was not physically present at the precise moment that any one of the Tate-LaBianca victims was killed. Yet his family swiftly murdered them on his orders, which, according to many later accounts, were meant to incite an apocalyptic race war that Mr. Manson called Helter Skelter. He took the name from the title of a Beatles song.

Throughout the decades since, Mr. Manson has remained an enigma. Was he a paranoid schizophrenic, as some observers have suggested? Was he a sociopath, devoid of human feeling? Was he a charismatic guru, as his followers once believed and his fans seemingly still do?

Or was he simply flotsam, a man whose life, The New York Times wrote in 1970, "stands as a monument to parental neglect and the failure of the public correctional system"?

No Name Maddox, as Mr. Manson was officially first known, was born on Nov. 12, 1934, to a 16-year-old unwed mother in Cincinnati. (Many accounts give the date erroneously as Nov. 11.) His mother, Kathleen Maddox, was often described as having been a prostitute. What is certain, according to Mr. Bugliosi's book and other accounts, is that she was a heavy drinker who lived on the margins of society with a series of men.

Mr. Manson apparently never knew his biological father. His mother briefly married another man, William Manson, and gave her young son the name Charles Milles Manson.

Kathleen often disappeared for long periods — when Charles was 5, for instance, she was sent to prison for robbing a gas station — leaving him to bounce among relatives in Ohio, West Virginia and Kentucky. She was paroled when Charles was 8 and took him back, but kept him for only a few years.

BURGLARY, ROBBERY, RAPE

From the age of 12 on, Charles was placed in a string of reform schools. At one institution, he held a razor to a boy's throat and raped him.

Escaping often, he committed burglaries, auto thefts and armed robberies, landing in between in juvenile detention centers and eventually federal reformatories. He was paroled from the last one at 19, in May 1954.

Starting in the mid-1950s, Mr. Manson, living mostly in Southern California, was variously a busboy, parking-lot attendant, car thief, check forger and pimp. During this period, he was in and out of prison.

He was married twice: in 1955 to Rosalie Jean Willis, a teenage waitress, and a few years later to a young prostitute named Leona. Both marriages ended in divorce.

Mr. Manson was believed to have fathered at least two children over the years: at least one with one of his wives, and at least one more with one of his followers. The precise number, names and whereabouts of his children — a subject around which rumor and urban legend have long coalesced — could not be confirmed.

By March 1967, when Mr. Manson, then 32, was paroled from his latest prison stay, he had spent more than half his life in correctional facilities. On his release, he moved to the Bay Area and eventually settled in the Haight-Ashbury district of San Francisco, the nerve center of hippiedom, just in time for the Summer of Love.

MIRRORPIX/GETTY IMAGES

Mr. Manson in 1980. He learned to play the guitar in prison and hoped to make it as a singer-songwriter.

There, espousing a philosophy that was an idiosyncratic mix of Scientology, hippie anti-authoritarianism, Beatles lyrics, the Book of Revelation and the writings of Hitler, he began to draw into his orbit the rootless young adherents who would become known as the Manson family.

Mr. Manson had learned to play the guitar in prison and hoped to make it as a singer-songwriter. His voice was once compared to that of the young Frankie Laine, a crooner who first became popular in the 1940s.

With his followers — a loose, shifting band of a dozen or more — Mr. Manson left San Francisco for Los Angeles. They stayed awhile in the home of Dennis Wilson, the Beach Boys' drummer. Mr. Manson hoped the association would help him land a recording contract, but none materialized. (The Beach Boys did later record a song, "Never Learn Not to Love," that was based on one written by Mr. Manson, although Mr. Wilson, who sang it, gave it new lyrics and a new title — Mr. Manson had called it "Cease to Exist" — and took credit for writing it.)

The Manson family next moved to the Spahn Movie Ranch, a mock Old West town north of Los Angeles that was once a film set but had since fallen to ruins. The group later moved to Death Valley, eventually settling at the Barker Ranch.

The desert location would protect the family, Mr. Manson apparently thought, in the clash of the races that he believed was inevitable. He openly professed his hatred of black people, and he believed that when Helter Skelter came, blacks would annihilate whites. Then, unable to govern themselves, the blacks would turn for leadership to the Manson family, who would have ridden out the conflict in deep underground holes in the desert.

A FRENZY OF BLOODSHED

At some point, Mr. Manson seems to have decided to help Helter Skelter along. Late at night on Aug. 8, 1969, he dispatched four family members — Susan Atkins, Patricia Krenwinkel, Charles Watson and Linda Kasabian — to the Tate home in the Hollywood hills. Mr. Manson knew the house: Terry Melcher, a well-known record producer with whom he had dealt fruitlessly, had once lived there.

Shortly after midnight on Aug. 9, Ms. Atkins, Ms. Krenwinkel and Mr. Watson entered the house while Ms. Kasabian waited outside. Through a frenzied combination of shooting, stabbing, beating and hanging, they murdered Ms. Tate and four others in the house and on the grounds: Jay Sebring, a Hollywood hairdresser; Abigail Folger, an heiress to the Folger coffee fortune; Voytek (also spelled Wojciech) Frykowski, Ms. Folger's boyfriend; and Steven Parent, an 18-year-old visitor. Ms. Tate's husband, Mr. Polanski, was in London at the time.

Before leaving, Ms. Atkins scrawled the word "pig" in blood on the front door of the house; in Mr. Manson's peculiar logic, the killings were supposed to look like the work of black militants.

The next night, Aug. 10, Mr. Manson and a half-dozen followers drove to a Los Angeles house he appeared to have selected at random. Inside, Mr. Manson tied up the residents — a wealthy grocer named Leno LaBianca and his wife, Rosemary — before leaving. After he was gone, several family members stabbed the couple to death. The phrases "Death to Pigs" and "Healter Skelter," misspelled, were scrawled in blood at the scene.

The seven murders went unsolved for months. Then, in the autumn of 1969, the police closed in on the Manson family after Ms. Atkins, in jail on an unrelated murder charge, bragged to cellmates about the killings.

On June 15, 1970, Mr. Manson, Ms. Atkins, Ms. Krenwinkel and a fourth family member, Leslie Van Houten, went on trial for murder. Ms. Kasabian, who had been present on both nights but said she had not participated in the killings, became the prosecution's star witness and was given immunity. Mr. Watson, who had fled to Texas, was tried and convicted separately.

During the trial, the bizarre became routine. On one occasion, Mr. Manson lunged at the judge with a pencil. On another, he punched his lawyer in open court. At one point, Mr. Manson appeared in court with an "X" carved into his forehead; his co-defendants quickly followed suit. (Mr. Manson later carved the X into a swastika, which remained flagrantly visible ever after.)

Outside the courthouse, a small flock of chanting family members kept vigil. One of them, Lynette Fromme, nicknamed Squeaky, would

BRIDE LANE LIBRARY/POPPERFOTO/GETTY IMAGES

On Jan. 25, 1971, the jury found Mr. Manson, Patricia Krenwinkel, left, and Susan Atkins, center, guilty of seven counts of murder each. Leslie Van Houten, right, was found guilty of two counts.

make headlines herself in 1975 when she tried to assassinate President Gerald R. Ford.

On Jan. 25, 1971, after nine days' deliberation, the jury found Mr. Manson, Ms. Atkins and Ms. Krenwinkel guilty of seven counts of murder each. Ms. Van Houten, who had been present only at the LaBianca murders, was found guilty of two counts. All four were also convicted of conspiracy to commit murder.

On March 29, the jury voted to give all four defendants the death penalty. In 1972, after capital punishment was temporarily outlawed in California, their sentences were reduced to life in prison.

Mr. Manson was convicted separately of two other murders: those of Gary Hinman, a musician killed by Manson family members in late July 1969, and Donald Shea, a Barker Ranch stuntman killed late that August. Altogether, Mr. Manson and seven family members were eventually convicted of one to nine murders apiece.

BETTMANN/GETTY IMAGES

Charles Manson being taken to jail months after the brutal killings of seven people in Los Angeles in 1969.

Incarcerated in a series of prisons over the years, Mr. Manson passed the time by playing the guitar, doing menial chores and making scorpions and spiders out of thread from his socks. His notoriety made him a target: In 1984, he was treated for second- and third-degree burns after being doused with paint thinner by a fellow inmate and set ablaze.

Mr. Manson was turned down for parole a dozen times, most recently in 2012. Most of the other convicted family members remain in prison. Ms. Atkins died in prison in 2009, at 61, of natural causes.

The Manson family was an inspiration for the television series "Aquarius," broadcast on NBC in 2015 and 2016. A period drama set in the late '60s, it starred David Duchovny as a Los Angeles police detective who comes up against Mr. Manson (played by the British actor Gethin Anthony) in the course of investigating a teenage girl's disappearance.

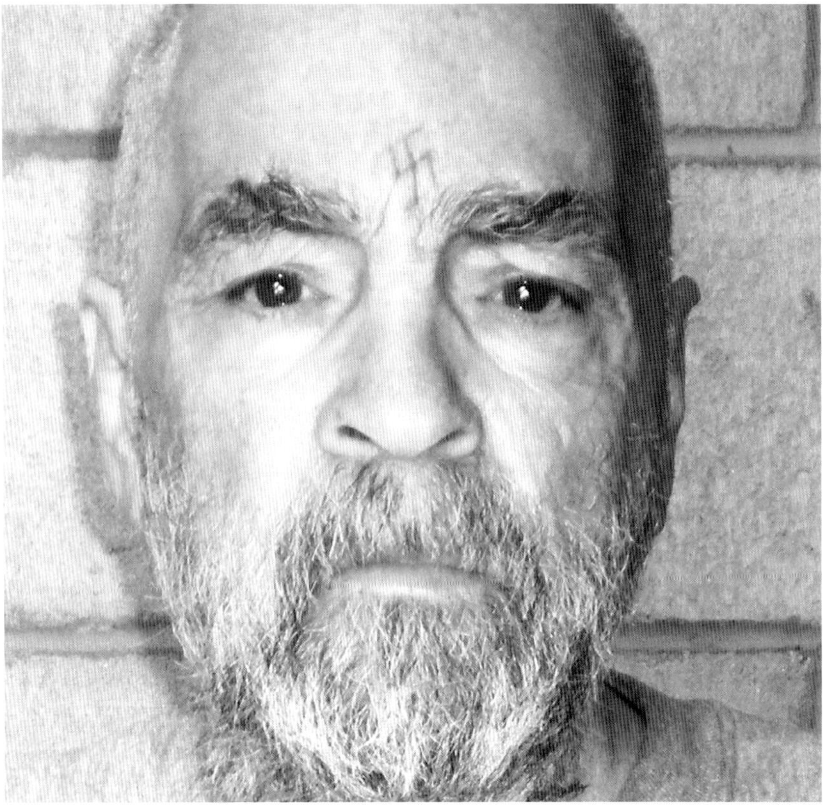

CALIFORNIA DEPARTMENT OF CORRECTIONS/GETTY IMAGES

Mr. Manson in a 2009 California Department of Corrections photo. To the end of his life, he denied having ordered the Tate-LaBianca murders. Nor, as he replied to a question he was often asked, did he feel remorse.

To the end of his life, Mr. Manson denied having ordered the Tate-LaBianca murders. Nor, as he replied to a question he was often asked, did he feel remorse, in any case.

He said as much in 1986 in a prison interview with the television journalist Charlie Rose.

"So you didn't care?" Mr. Rose asked, invoking Ms. Tate and her unborn child.

"Care?" Mr. Manson replied.

He added, "What the hell does that mean, 'care'?"

What Became of the Manson Family?

BY AMISHA PADNANI | NOV. 20, 2017

OVER TWO NIGHTS in August 1969, Charles Manson's followers savagely murdered seven people through a frenzied combination of shooting, stabbing, beating and hanging.

Their most famous victim was the actress Sharon Tate, the wife of the film director Roman Polanski. She was killed at her house along with four guests. The following night, the gang murdered a wealthy grocer named Leno LaBianca and his wife, Rosemary.

At their trial, members of the so-called Manson family shamelessly admitted their crimes and flaunted their allegiance to a leader whom they said they loved and who was portrayed as controlling their minds.

Most of his followers were young women who had fled middle-class and upper-class homes to live with Mr. Manson at the Spahn Movie Ranch, a mock Old West town near Los Angeles that was once a film set but had fallen into ruin. One sang in her church choir. Another recalled being enchanted by Mr. Manson through what she hoped was a budding romance.

Mr. Manson, who died on Sunday, and four members of his gang were sentenced to death. In 1972, their sentences were reduced to life in prison when capital punishment was outlawed in California. (It was reinstated in 1978.)

Here is a look at what happened to some of his most ardent followers.

SUSAN ATKINS

Ms. Atkins was a quiet middle-class girl who was born in San Gabriel, Calif. She has said that her parents were alcoholics and that she was sexually abused by a male relative. She sang in her school's glee club and her church choir, but she quit high school and left home when she was 18. She met Mr. Manson soon after, and he gave her a new name, Sadie Mae Glutz.

RALPH CRANE/THE LIFE PICTURE COLLECTION/GETTY IMAGES

Susan Atkins in 1969.

In 1968, she gave birth to a son. Mr. Manson — who by all accounts was not the father — had her name the child Zezozose Zadfrack Glutz. The child was eventually removed from Ms. Atkins's care and later adopted.

Ms. Atkins was arrested in October 1969 in the murder of Gary Hinman, a friend of Mr. Manson's, and convicted. At that point, the police did not know who was responsible for the Tate-LaBianca murders. But Ms. Atkins implicated herself in jail, when she is said to have admitted to cellmates that she stabbed Ms. Tate, tasted her blood and used it to write "Pig" on the front door of the house.

Ms. Atkins became a born-again Christian in 1974 while in prison, she wrote in her memoir, "Child of Satan, Child of God" (with Bob Slosser). She denounced Mr. Manson, formed a prison ministry and did charitable work of all kinds. She was routinely denied parole and died at a women's prison in Chowchilla, Calif., in 2009, at 61, a year after she was found to have brain cancer.

BETTMANN/GETTY IMAGES

Patricia Krenwinkel in 1970.

PATRICIA KRENWINKEL

Ms. Krenwinkel was a 19-year-old secretary from Los Angeles when she met Mr. Manson at a party. Three days later, she said, she left everything behind to pursue a romantic relationship with him.

She said during her trial that at Ms. Tate's home, she chased down Abigail Anne Folger, the heiress of the coffee fortune. "We fought on the grass," she testified. "I remember stabbing her, stabbing and stabbing."

She said she also assisted in the killings of the LaBiancas the following night.

Ms. Krenwinkel, now 69, has been in a women's prison in Corona, Calif., for about 47 years, longer than any other woman in the state. She has been denied parole at least 13 times.

"The saddest part is my definition of love was totally skewed," she said in a 2014 documentary, "Life After Manson."

BETTMANN/GETTY IMAGES

Leslie Van Houten in 1970.

LESLIE VAN HOUTEN

Ms. Van Houten said she recalled stabbing Mrs. LaBianca in the abdomen 14 to 16 times. She showed little remorse in court as she described wiping away fingerprints and burning her clothing. She said she remembered taking chocolate milk and cheese from the refrigerator before leaving.

Many years later, Ms. Van Houten, calm and articulate, was regarded as a model prisoner at a women's prison in Corona, Calif. She said that she regretted taking part in the murders and that at the time she had been mentally ill, a condition aggravated by LSD use.

"I believed that he was Jesus Christ," Ms. Van Houten said of Mr. Manson. "I bought into it lock, stock and barrel."

Ms. Van Houten, 68, was granted parole in September after she was denied at least 20 times.

ROLLS PRESS/POPPERFOTO/GETTY IMAGES

Linda Kasabian in 1970.

LINDA KASABIAN

Ms. Kasabian, who was 20 at the time of the murders, became the prosecution's star witness and was given immunity. She said that she kept watch on both nights and that she had not participated in the killings.

She was raised in New Hampshire and moved to Los Angeles to live with the man she married. She said she joined Mr. Manson's family in July 1969 after feeling rejected by her husband.

In her testimony, she said Mr. Manson was the Devil and that she did not report him to the police because she feared for the safety of her daughter.

After the trial, she returned to New Hampshire. She is 68.

BETTMANN/GETTY IMAGES

Charles Watson in 1970.

CHARLES WATSON

Known as Tex, Mr. Watson, a lanky former honor student and high school athlete from Dallas, was said to have led the killing spree as Mr. Manson's assistant after living at the Spahn Ranch for parts of 1968 and 1969.

After the murders, he fled to his native Texas, where he was arrested, and fought extradition for so long that the other members of Mr. Manson's family were tried without him. When he was finally extradited, he pleaded guilty by reason of insanity from overuse of hallucinogenic drugs, but was deemed fit for trial and convicted of murder.

In recent decades, Mr. Watson, now 71, is said to have fathered four children from conjugal visits in prison, and he has founded a prison-cell ministry. He was denied parole for the 17th time in 2016 and remains at Mule Creek State Prison in Ione, Calif.

Charles Manson's Remains Will Go to Purported Grandson, Judge Rules

BY MATTHEW HAAG | MARCH 12, 2018

JASON L. FREEMAN, a purported grandson of Charles Manson, claimed in court papers that he was the notorious killer's true heir.

He wanted to give him a proper burial, Mr. Freeman said in a recent interview, noting that he would invite a small "inner circle" of his grandfather's friends to a private funeral service and then spread his ashes over water.

Now, it appears, Mr. Freeman will get that chance.

In a messy legal battle over Mr. Manson's remains and belongings, a judge in Kern County, Calif., ruled on Monday that Mr. Freeman, a Florida man who had claimed that his father was Mr. Manson's son, was the "surviving competent adult next of kin." Three other men who had also staked claims — a purported friend who said he filed Mr. Manson's will in court; and two people, including a purported son, who filed a joint petition — could not refute Mr. Freeman's assertion, the judge said.

Mr. Freeman, who could not be reached for comment on Monday evening, said in an interview in January: "I'd like to grab ahold of my grandfather's name and have a little more control over it. Everybody's had a free-for-all for the past 50 years."

The ruling on Monday capped the first part of what has become a complicated tug-of-war over what Mr. Manson left behind, which some have speculated would probably not be much beyond his body. The order, which was issued by Judge Alisa R. Knight of the Bakersfield Division of the Superior Court of California, addressed only who could take Mr. Manson's body, which has been held in a storage facility in Kern County since his death at 83 on Nov. 19 while serving a sentence of life in prison.

Dale A. Kiken, a lawyer for Mr. Freeman, said the ruling would bring closure to Mr. Freeman. He said his client had struggled with his

BRIAN MELLEY/ASSOCIATED PRESS

Jason Freeman, the purported grandson of Mr. Manson, has said he wants to give Mr. Manson a "proper burial" by spreading his ashes.

family's history, saying that Mr. Freeman's father, Charles Manson Jr., who killed himself in 1993, was also not someone he admired.

"He's trying to deal with that in his own way, and part of that is bringing part of the episode to a close," Mr. Kiken said in an interview on Monday night. "That's a pretty big burden."

The second part of the legal battle, over the heir to Mr. Manson's personal belongings, was expected to continue in Los Angeles Superior Court this week.

Throughout his life, Mr. Manson acquired a bizarre celebrity status, attracting fanatical followers, pen pals and collectors of his jail-cell creations. In some ways, the legal battle after his death has mirrored Mr. Manson's mystifying grip on American pop culture that he held long after the brutal killings by his followers, known as the Tate-LaBianca murders, on two consecutive nights in August 1969.

“There is a lot of notoriety around Mr. Manson, and there still remains a cadre of peoples who hold him in high esteem,” Mr. Kiken said.

The first person who filed a claim for Mr. Manson’s remains was Michael Channels, a longtime pen pal with him, who said the killer gave him a will in 2002 that left everything to Mr. Channels. But Judge Knight wrote in her ruling that the will presented by Mr. Channels did not meet California’s legal requirements.

The other petition was filed by Benjamin Gurecki and Matthew Lentz and claimed that Mr. Lentz was Mr. Manson’s son. But because Mr. Lentz was adopted after he was born, he forfeited any relationship with his biological parents, Judge Knight ruled.

Mr. Kiken said Mr. Freeman planned to travel to California within the next week to receive Mr. Manson’s body. In the meantime, the next legal phase moves to Los Angeles, where the same four men have made claims for his belongings.

But it is unclear what Mr. Manson, who was sentenced to prison in 1971 on seven counts of first-degree murder, left to be collected.

“What has a guy who has been in jail for 50 years have to his name?” Mr. Kiken said. “I couldn’t begin to value what is there.”

MATT STEVENS contributed reporting.

CHAPTER 2

Jim Jones: The People's Temple

Jim Jones was an idealist. He believed in Marxism and racial integration, in free speech and helping the community. He was an ordained minister. And he orchestrated the murder-suicides of 909 people. Leader of The People's Temple, Jones and hundreds of ardent followers built a largely self-sufficient settlement called Jonestown in Guyana. But it was not the paradise it was purported to be. When stories of sexual and emotional abuse and other human rights violations surfaced, Jones ordered his entire congregation — including 304 children — to swallow cyanide-laced grape drink mix. And they did.

Pastor a Charlatan to Some, a Philosopher to Wife

BY WALLACE TURNER | SEPT. 2, 1977

SAN FRANCISCO, SEPT. 1 — No matter what others say, to his wife, Jim Jones is a Marxist social philosopher and pastor to whom "service to my fellow man is the highest service to God."

But in a flood of recent publicity, Mr. Jones has been pictured as a charlatan who victimizes those whose religious faith he captures, taking their property, physically abusing them and using them as pawns in his political power games.

Mr. Jones, 46 years old, resigned his appointive position as chairman of the San Francisco Housing Authority after the criticism began. District attorneys in San Francisco and Mendocino Counties are checking allegations of irregularities in property transfers. The California Secretary of State's office is checking allegations that notaries public improperly endorsed some transfer documents.

These are the most serious charges made to date, although there have also been allegations of physical mistreatment, such as disciplinary paddlings, and the use of shoddy tricks to impress members of his congregation.

FORMER MEMBERS QUOTED

The trouble for Mr. Jones and his 9,000-member church was made public two months ago in an article in New West magazine. The article quoted former members who told about their disaffection. Then both San Francisco dailies, The Chronicle and The Examiner, printed articles on the matter.

Throughout all this, Mr. Jones, a Butler University graduate and United Church of Christ minister for 25 years, has been unavailable. Marceline Jones, his wife of 28 years, said in an interview this week that he was at the church's agricultural mission, a 27,000-acre jungle tract on the northeast coast of South America at Guyana.

Beyond issuing blanket denials of wrongdoing, Mr. Jones has not discussed the charges, nor have members of his congregation.

A registered nurse, Mrs. Jones worked for 10 years for the California State Board of Health until resigning Aug. 1 for reasons, she said, of health and because of pressing duties at the temple. In the interview, she described her husband as a Marxist who holds religion's trappings to be useful chiefly for social and economic uplift.

"Jim has used religion to try to get some people out of the opiate of religion," she said. She quoted him as saying to her, "Marcie, I've got to destroy this paper idol," as he slammed down the Bible he held in his hand.

They were married in 1949, when he was 19 and she was 22. They have one natural son, Stephen Gandhi Jones, and seven adopted children who are black, Korean, Indian and Caucasian.

"I wanted to come to California because the multiracial nature of our family was a problem in Indiana," she said. "But we've had problems here, too."

With 120 followers, they moved in 1965 from Indianapolis to Ukiah, Calif. Five years ago they opened the church here in an old building in a black slum. The agricultural project opened four years ago.

In an interview a year ago, Mr. Jones said that his congregation was 40 percent Caucasian, 40 percent black and 20 percent a mixture of Oriental, Indian and Chicano. He is of Welsh and Indian extraction, and Mrs. Jones is Caucasian.

The congregation is activist. A year ago 1,200 members picketed the Fresno County Courthouse while four employees of The Fresno Bee were held in jail for refusing to identify their news sources.

Mr. Jones said then that the temple supported many causes to protect newspaper sources. He said of the Fresno pickets, "I can't stand to see our press crippled. Who else would take a stand? Our duty is to be here."

Mr. Jones's alleged political strength has been emphasized in the newspaper accounts of temple affairs. The published names have been mostly those of liberal Democrats such as Mayor George Moscone, who appointed Mr. Jones as chairman of the housing authority; Assemblyman Willie Brown, and Sheriff Richard Hongisto. All have been supported by the temple at election time and have appeared at temple meetings.

However, the record also shows that the pastor has sought to establish friendships and dialogue with other leaders, including officials of the John Birch Society who have also spoken at temple meetings.

One of Mr. Jones's techniques for gaining attention has been to make substantial contributions by checks to newspaper publishers, saying that the money was to support press freedom. In this way, he became known to the late Charles Theriot, publisher of, The

Chronicle, who sent the money to Sigma Delta Chi, a national journalism organization.

The pastor's aim, according to his wife, is to provide a communal life for all his members. "We live by the rule of from each according to his ability and to each according to his need," she said. Funds are pooled, she said, with medical care, dental care, housing and food, educational expenses and church expenses paid from the common purse.

The temple has educated a medical doctor who now is interning in Guyana, she said. A dentist educated by the temple is among the former members whose criticisms are the basis for some of the temple's unfavorable publicity, she said.

Mr. Jones's Marxist twist to religion came to him when he was about 21 years old, his wife said. She said that he told her then that "in order to bring people out of their superstition you have to give them a substitute." She recalled that he pointed out that Jesus told the rich man, "Sell what you have and give it to the poor."

Mrs. Jones was asked if she contributed her salary to the temple when she worked for the state. She did not.

"Jim and I have long felt that if they didn't assassinate him, they'd try to get him by law," she said. "I put my checks in a special fund so Jim could have the best legal counsel."

Dispute Over Baby Spurred Sect's Move to Guyana

BY WALLACE TURNER | NOV. 19, 1978

SAN FRANCISCO, NOV. 18 — The People's Temple, the religious group being investigated by Representative Leo J. Ryan when he was shot today in Guyana, is led by the Rev. Jim Jones, a 47-year-old white man who describes himself as part Indian.

His group includes many blacks, Asians and American Indians as well as whites. It was organized from an old church building in a poor section of San Francisco and caters mostly to the people who live in that area.

Mr. Jones's wife, Marceline, a registered nurse, said last year that he never was a true believer in Christianity but instead a Marxist who hoped to use Christian fundamentalism as a means to bring potential followers into his orbit where he could influence them to support his aims.

CHAIRMAN OF HOUSING AUTHORITY

Mr. Jones methodically found ways to make himself helpful to political figures in San Francisco. His loyalty and support to state Senator George Moscone were rewarded when Mr. Moscone was elected Mayor in 1975. Mr. Jones was appointed chairman of the San Francisco Housing Authority.

Before coming to San Francisco, he had founded his religious group in Mendecino County, a predominantly rural area on the coast north of here. Some of those who joined him in Mendecino County later left the group.

A child born to a married woman created problems for Mr. Jones. His attorney, Charles Garry, in an interview last year, said the child was the chief reason that Mr. Jones left here to go to Guyana.

The mother and her husband had sought to have the child's custody

BRIDE LANE LIBRARY/POPPERFOTO/GETTY IMAGES

Jim Jones in 1975.

restored to them when they left the People's Temple. Instead Mr. Jones had the child sent to Guyana.

COUPLE SOUGHT CHILD'S RETURN

Mr. Garry said he had been told that Mr. Jones was the father of the child. The mother and her husband denied this and pressed vigorously for the return of the child to their custody.

About 18 months ago, newspaper and magazine articles depicted Mr. Jones as having defrauded and misled members of his church. Strange practices, including sometimes brutal beatings, were described.

Quickly, Mr. Jones resigned the housing authority post, and left to visit the communal colony he had established at a tract of land he had acquired and named Jonestown in Guyana.

Political pressure by Mr. Jones's former colleagues eventually prompted Representative Ryan to organize the flight to Guyana, and he took reporters from each of San Francisco's newspapers with him.

On arrival in Georgetown, Guyana, The San Francisco Chronicle's man was held 13 hours at the airport in an immigration inquiry.

The newspaper reported here today that Representative Ryan, whose district includes northern San Mateo County and part of San Francisco, had led members of the party to Jonestown and that a full description of that visit would be printed in the next few days.

Deaths in Guyana Threaten Sect's California Organization

BY WALLACE TURNER | NOV. 20, 1978

SAN FRANCISCO, NOV. 19 — The powerful political-religious organization that the Rev. Jim Jones built as the People's Temple seemed today to be in danger of breaking apart in the aftermath of five murders at the airstrip that serves the group's agricultural colony at Jonestown, Guyana.

Services have been held at 11 A.M. each Sunday for several years at the group's meeting place, a three-story brick structure on the edge of the Fillmore slum, but there were no services today. The doors were locked, and the police were called to restrain a woman relative of one Jonestown resident.

Just after 11 A.M., Archie Ijames, a black man who identified himself as a minister, came out to the rainswept steps with two stone-faced men, one white and one black. He read a statement that said there had been no radio contact with Jonestown since yesterday morning by church groups here or in Los Angeles or Georgetown, Guyana.

Jonestown sits in a remote area of Guyana, a nation on the northeast coast of South America whose capital is Georgetown.

JONES IS SAID TO 'DEPLORE VIOLENCE'

Mr. Ijames's statement disavowed violence and expressed condolences to families of the five persons who were killed and those who were wounded in the shooting at dusk yesterday on the airstrip at Port Kaituma, Guyana.

"Rev. Jim Jones has always deplored violence," Mr. Ijames said, "and whatever the circumstances of the airstrip incident it is not the kind of action anyone within the temple ever would precipitate. The statement called "sensational and patently untrue" the State Department suggestion of mass suicide among temple members.

The People's Temple has prospered in money, members and political influence — ever since Mr. Jones moved his flock of 100 from Indianapolis to Redwood Valley, near Ukiah, Calif., in 1965. The temple moved here in 1971 but began to decline in the summer of 1977, when news reports critical of the temple appeared, and Mr. Jones went to Guyana.

The church work continued but the political influence declined, and large sums of money were moved into the jungle-reclamation project. Many members went there to live.

ORIGINALLY FROM LYNN, IND.

Membership in the temple reached high of 10,000 in 1976, Mr. Jones said. It was predominantly black, but with large white, Asian and American Indian groups. The 47-year-old Mr. Jones, a native of Lynn, Ind., and a graduate of Butler University, said he is "all American mongrel, part Indian, part Welsh."

His political power was based on the fact that, at a nod from Mr. Jones, hundreds — even thousands — of church members turned out to campaign and vote. A man of what one official described as "hypnotic charisma," Mr. Jones was skillful in using this power to influence the power centers he needed.

For example, when four employees of a California newspaper, The Fresno Bee, were jailed in September 1976 for refusing to name the sources of news stories, busloads of People's Temple members arrived to picket the courthouse. In visits with reporters, Mr. Jones described his dedication to the principles of a free press.

He invited political and civic leaders to the church, where enthusiastic crowds greeted them with apparently spontaneous displays of support. Later, disaffected members said Mr. Jones orchestrated those displays, but they did help him build a strong political base.

COMPLAINTS FROM FORMER MEMBERS

Then in the summer of 1977, New West magazine printed an attack on Mr. Jones and the People's Temple. The attack was based on statements of former members who said the pastor performed spurious miracles that were outright trickery, that physical and mental anguish was used to enforce compliance with his orders and that members were encouraged to turn over all they owned to the temple.

Mr. Jones denied everything. The district attorney's office here could find no chargeable offense, although it closely examined many sales of homes that had been donated to the temple. Nevertheless, Mr. Jones resigned as chairman of the San Francisco Housing Authority which his friend, Mayor George Moscone had appointed him. In August 1977, he left for Guyana.

Mr. Jones's wife of 29 years, Marceline, is a nurse whom he married when he was 18 years old and she was a 22-year-old student nurse. In an interview a year ago, she recalled that when Mr. Jones was 18, Mao Tse-tung was his hero. By the time he was about 21, she said, he realized that in order to bring people out of their superstition, "you have to give them a substitute."

The substitute was religion — in which Mr. Jones did not believe, his wife said. His aim was a Marxist social group, and that was what he was building in Guyana. But Mrs. Jones insisted that her husband is a man dedicated to the welfare of his church members and mankind.

Government sources have said that about 1,000 passport applications were filed here for temple members going to Guyana. It was the welfare of these members that concerned Representative Leo J. Ryan and led him to make the inspection trip to Jonestown that ended in his death yesterday.

Relatives of some of the Jonestown residents moved warily around the temple today, talking to reporters and trying to find out what is happening in Guyana. Most were unwilling to identify themselves.

A 25-year-old black woman said her mother and sister went to Jonestown eight months ago. She had a recent letter, she said, that was signed by her mother but was not written in her mother's handwriting. It seemed to her to have been written by someone else in order to quiet her concerns.

Defectors From Sect Depict Its Rehearsals for Suicide

BY ROBERT LINDSEY | NOV. 21, 1978

LOS ANGELES, NOV. 20 — "He has mass suicide drills, where he tells all the people, hundreds of people, to drink a certain drink, and he says, 'That's fatal, you're all going to die in 45 minutes, want to see how you feel about dying for socialism.' "

And, said Timothy Stoen, a San Francisco lawyer and former aide to the Rev. Jim Jones, the founder of the People's Temple, when Mr. Jones ordered his followers in his Guyana commune to drink the liquid, "everybody drank."

"It was like he wanted to believe he was God," said Anna Mobley, a member for four years. "He would get you so tired it would make you lose your mind."

"He had something they called the 'blue-eyed monster,' a thing they did to children," another former member said. "They took children into a dark room and attached electrodes to them and then shocked them and told them never not to smile at Jim Jones."

"He sent spies to our home and said that if we didn't sell all our property, we would die," said Wade Medlock, the owner of a Los Angeles maintenance company, who turned over two of his homes to the cult under threats.

The remarks were made at a meeting of a group called the Human Freedom Foundation, which was set up here last summer by two psychics, Maria Papaperos and Jenita Cargile, after former cult members had sought them out for counseling on how to "deprogram" themselves. A recording of the meeting was made available to The New York Times.

According to former members, the cult was run as a police state by Mr. Jones, who was said to have enforced discipline by beatings and death threats, pursued bizarre sexual activities, and indoctrinated members in his personal brand of agrarian socialism.

According to Mr. Stoen, Mr. Jones first enticed members with a doctrine of selflessness and a simple Christian faith of social equality that found support among blacks and upper middle-class whites who had become alienated in the 1960's.

Once he got "control of their minds, he would accept no dissent and told members that a defector had no right to live," Mr. Stoen said. He is a former deputy district attorney in Mendocino County who had been attracted by Mr. Jones's views in the late 1960's and became one of his lieutenants as the cult spread to San Francisco and Los Angeles and ultimately to the settlement in Guyana.

He said that as a sect official he had transferred more than $5 million to foreign bank accounts and said he believed the church's assets probably totaled much more.

Mr. Stoen said "people who disagreed would get phone calls at 3 A.M. with heavy breathing" or cult officials would find a drunk and pay him to read a script containing threats over the telephone. The children of parents who decided to leave the sect were often seized and kept in Guyana under guard.

Mr. Jones, he continued, had a "relationships committee" that had to approve all romantic entanglements among members. Once, Mr. Stoen said, there was a young woman who had been seeing a male cult member, and Mr. Jones forced her to engage in sexual relationships with another man before all 1,100 members of the commune.

"He was always talking about sex," Mr. Stoen said about the sect leader.

According to this account, Mr. Jones encouraged men and women to live in separate quarters. Married couples who insisted on staying together were required to live in bunk beds with a blanket providing their only privacy.

Mr. Stoen said Mr. Jones was "paranoid and always afraid," and turned away relatives of commune members. When newcomers arrived, he seized passport and money, holding them virtual prisoners, Mr. Stoen said.

Mr. Jones, he said, planned several escape routes from Guyana because he believed that the authorities might someday invade his commune and he "expected to go out with a splash."

LAWSUIT DEPOSITION IS QUOTED

Allegations about the oppressive nature of Mr. Jones's leadership have emerged in lawsuits in California. One former member of the sect, Deborah Layton Blakey, said about Mr. Jones in a suit filed in San Franciso:

"He convinced Temple members that if they did not follow him to Guyana, they would be put into concentration camps and killed. White members were instilled with the belief that their names appeared on a secret list of enemies that was kept by the C.I.A. and that they would be tracked down, tortured, imprisoned and killed if they didn't flee to Guyana.

"At various times, Rev. Jones claimed that he was the reincarnation of either Lenin, Jesus Christ, or one of a variety of other religious or political figures. He claimed that he had divine powers and healed the sick. He stated that he had extrasensory perception and could tell what everyone was thinking. He said that he had powerful connections the world over, including the Mafia, Idi Amin and the Soviet Government."

Leader of Sect Dies

BY JON NORDHEIMER | NOV. 21, 1978

GEORGETOWN, GUYANA, NOV. 23 — In a scene that dashed the senses, Guyanese forces today picked their way through an open-air pavilion choked with the bodies of 405 men, women and children in an American cult group who apparently committed suicide on the orders of their leader.

Wearing gaily colored clothes, the bodies were clustered in family groups, side-by-side in deathly embrace, all but three dead from drinking a concoction made of Kool-Aid and cyanide.

The setting was the jungle church of the People's Temple, the group that has been blamed for the slaying of Congressman Leo J. Ryan and four other Americans on Saturday.

SURVIVOR DESCRIBES SCENE

A surviving cult member gave the first newsmen to reach the scene today an account that was as incredible as it was filled with horror, a story of death plots and madness, of parents spooning a poisonous punch into the mouths of their babies before drinking it themselves.

And on the altar of the pavilion, surrounded in death by his followers as he had been surrounded by them in life, was the body of James Warren Jones, also known as the Rev. Jim Jones, the charismatic leader of the People's Temple, who had promised his racially integrated flock a utopia in the South American wilds. Instead, he gave them death.

"The time has come to meet in another place," he was said to have told the cultists he had assembled around him shortly after learning of the failure of a plan to kill the entire group of newsmen and parents of cultists who had flown deep into a lonely jungle airport with Congressman Ryan, according to the survivor, Odell Rhodes, 36 years old, from Detroit.

TIM CHAPMAN/HULTON ARCHIVE/GETTY IMAGES

The bodies of hundreds of people who dropped where they were after drinking cyanide-laced grape drink mix.

400 ARE STILL MISSING

And then, according to the survivor's account, cyanide was dumped into a huge soup kettle, and the liquid was fed first to the babies, then to the children old enough to drink it themselves, and finally swallowed by the adults, many of whom were older people who had turned their Social Security checks and their lives over to the custody of Mr. Jones.

The leader, who at different times had described himself as the reincarnation of Christ and Lenin, died of a bullet wound in the head, according to the Guyanese police.

Nothing is known about the whereabouts of the remaining 900 or more cultists, who either fled into the jungle to escape death, or have elected to die deeper inside the canopied rain forest, where flesh-eating piranha and electric eels move in the murky jungle streams and insects swarm in the midday heat.

CULT WAS DRILLED IN SUICIDE

It was learned that the cult was routinely drilled in suicide by Mr. Jones, who had a vision of a need to destroy the community if it was ever attacked.

Apparently, Mr. Ryan, who had been asked to investigate claims by his California constituents that members of the cult were being held in virtual bondage on the commune, and the party that accompanied him last Saturday, were seen as a grave danger.

Mr. Jones had decided to kill Mr. Ryan and the two dozen or so people who accompanied him, according to Mr. Rhodes. The plan was to send one of his loyal lieutenants with the Ryan party as a feigned defector. When the plane was airborne, the accomplice was to kill the pilot and cause a crash in the dense jungle.

The plan was nearly carried out. But the imposter boarded the smaller of the two chartered planes at the small airstrip at Port Kaituma, and for some unexplained reason began shooting while both planes were still on the ground. At this time a tractor emerged from the jungle carrying several men who opened fire on the confused, scrambling Americans, killing Mr. Ryan, two members of a National Broadcasting Company crew, a photographer for the San Francisco Examiner and one of the defecting cultists. Eight others were wounded.

Mr. Rhodes said that an assembly of the People's Temple was called by Mr. Jones before the results of what was transpiring at the airport, six miles away, were known. He told them of his plot to kill Mr. Ryan's entourage and protect the cult from further intrusions.

MEMBERS DIED IN FAMILY GROUPS

When word came back that the plan had been botched and survivors had escaped on one of the aircraft, Mr. Jones announced that he was invoking his ultimate plan.

Armed guards ringed the assembly as a physician, Lawrence Schact, prepared the cyanide punch, but they were not needed to coerce the true believers, according to Mr. Rhodes. They lined up in family groups, he said, took their drinks, put their arms around each other, had convulsions and died within five minutes.

Mr. Jones's legal wife and son died with him on the altar. His mistress, Maria Katsaris, whose mother was one of those wounded in the airport shooting, apparently shot herself in the head in a nearby cabin after apparently feeding cyanide to the two small boys she and Mr. Jones treated like sons. Eighty-two children in all died that day.

40 WEAPONS AND $500,000 FOUND

A search of the settlement turned up nearly 40 weapons, including some automatic rifles and "hundreds of thousands of rounds of ammunition," according to Guyanese police investigators.

In addition, there was approximately $500,000 in United States currency and many United States Treasury checks. A former cult member who had worked as financial secretary for the People's Temple had indicated several months ago that Mr. Jones received $65,000 a month in Social Security checks turned over to him by his older followers. More than 800 American passports were found at the settlement, and the authorities are not certain if that is the number of Americans who lived there. Earlier estimates had placed the number closer to 1,200.

Six individuals who had been on the plane at the airstrip Saturday when the shooting broke out and who had fled into the jungle turned up yesterday. One, Jim Cobb, was a Californian who had flown into the jungle with Mr. Ryan. The other five, ages 5 to 20 years old, were being taken out of the settlement at the time of the incident. Two of the children were wounded slightly. In addition, the authorities located two adult cult members who said they had not been involved in any of the deaths. They were identified as Michael Prokes, a former television newsman in California, and Tim Carter. The authorities also hold the man suspected of starting the shooting at the airstrip, Larry Layton. All were being held for questioning.

NEW YORK TIMES CO./NEAL BOENZI/GETTY IMAGES

Members of a U.S. military team prepare aluminum coffins for shipment to the United States, following the more than 900 deaths in the mass suicide staged in Jonestown by members of the People's Temple and their leader, the Reverend Jim Jones.

BODIES FLOWN TO U.S.

Two lawyers who had represented the group, Mark Lane, the author, and Charles Garry, a San Francisco lawyer, escaped from the group's village of Jonestown on Saturday night when the killings began and were picked up in the jungle by Government forces yesterday They did not see the killings.

The bodies of Mr. Ryan and the four others killed with him were flown back to the United States today after a post mortem in Georgetown, the capital city.

Tomorrow, 50 American mortuary experts are scheduled to be flown to the interior to begin identifying the 405 dead cult members whose bodies have been exposed to the tropical heat for more than two days. In addition, the United States is expected to provide the Guyanese with military helicopters to airlift the bodies to Georgetown.

Congressman Ryan had met with Mr. Jones on Saturday at the commune, called Jonestown, to negotiate for the release of cult members whose parents in California had claimed were being held in virtual bondage.

Besides Mr. Ryan, who was 53 years old, those killed Saturday were Don Harris, 42, a television reporter for NBC News, and Robert Brown, 36, an NBC cameraman, both of Los Angeles; Gregory Robinson, 27, a photographer for The San Francisco Examiner, and Patricia Parks, a cult member. Guyanese officials said she was 18 years old.

In addition, it was reported today that a People's Temple leader, Sharon Amos, and her three daughters had been found with their throats slit in the cult's headquarters in Georgetown.

The Guyanese Minister of Information, Shirley Field-Ridley, today expressed her Government's sympathy to the relatives of the dead Americans, saying her South American country had never experienced anything like the "very terrible happenings" of the weekend.

WARNINGS ABOUT VIOLENCE

Former members of the cult had warned that it was capable of violence. Last June, one former member, Deborah Layton Blakey, said in a deposition in a Guyana custody case involving a child in the Jonestown commune: "The Rev. Jones labeled any person who left the commune a 'traitor' and 'fair game.' He steadfastly and convincingly maintained that the punishment for defection was death."

"There was constant talk of death," said Mrs. Blakey, who was raised in an affluent family in Berkeley, Calif. "In Jonestown, the concept of mass suicide for socialism arose. Because our lives were so wretched anyway, and because we were so afraid to contradict Rev. Jones, the concept was not challenged."

NIGHT MEETINGS DESCRIBED

According to her account, states of emergency called "white nights" were declared about once a week and followed this routine:

Sirens woke everyone and about 50 guards with rifles rushed around the settlement corralling everyone to a mass meeting. The members were told that some enemy, like mercenaries controlled by the Central Intelligence Agency, was in the jungle and would overrun the camp and that death was imminent.

"During a 'white night' we were informed that our situation was hopeless and that the only course of action open to us was a mass suicide for the glory of socialism," she said. "We were told everyone would he tortured by the mercenaries if we were taken alive. Everyone, including the children, were told to line up. As we passed through the line we were given a small glass of red liquid to drink. We were told the liquid contained poison and we would die within 15 minutes. We all did as we were told."

When no one fell ill or died, Mr. Jones explained that what they had drunk was not poison: he was just putting them through a "loyalty test."

"He warned us that the time was not far off when it would become necessary for us to die by our own hands."

Cult Chief's Beginnings in Indianapolis Recalled

BY JAMES FERON | NOV. 22, 1978

NYACK, N.Y., NOV. 21 — As a young churchman in Indianapolis the Rev. Jim Jones was "an obviously intelligent, eager, concerned person of great initiative" who lived simply, organized soup kitchens and nursing homes, and helped minorities, a former church leader recalled today.

"That was in the 1950's, when Jim Jones first came to public attention," said Barton Hunter, executive director of the 16,000-member Fellowship of Reconciliation, a 65-year-old pacifist organization.

A decade later, however, Mr. Jones was the leader of a new People's Temple and was "healing" the ill instead of simply caring for them, recruiting minority members to his church rather than just welcoming them, and reaching beyond local concerns to grapple with larger issues.

The charismatic leader had taken on a messianic role and, with 70 families who gave up their jobs and homes, he left for California because of what he felt was harassment in Indiana. In another decade he would move with an even larger group to Guyana, feeling that his group was harassed in California.

'COSMIC PROPORTIONS'

Mr. Jones had "come to see himself in cosmic proportions" even in Indianapolis, Mr. Hunter said. Last weekend the cult leader led hundreds of members of his cult into suicide after the slaying of Representative Leo J. Ryan and four other Americans who visited the jungle site of the People's Temple.

"You ask yourself, 'What happened? Where did it all go wrong?' " Mr. Hunter said in an interview at the converted Hudson River mansion that serves as headquarters of his fellowship. His wife, Dorothy, sat at his side, and Mr. Hunter recalled their first meeting with Mr. Jones:

"I was executive secretary of the Church in Society of the Christian Church, Disciples of Christ, and a social worker who was a member of our congregation said, 'I'd like you to meet a young man; he has similar interests.'

"He was a minister, a Methodist pastor, with a congregation that included small ecstatic group of people. He was involved in peace and social justice and he was in touch with depressed people. He lived with them," Mr. Hunter said.

Eventually, Mr. Hunter said, Mr. Jones withdrew from the Methodist fold and set up his own temple in a former synagogue on North Delaware Street in Indianapolis. His congregation, consisting of more black than white members, began to appeal also to fringe groups.

SYNAGOGUE PURCHASED

Mr. Jones purchased the building from a congregation headed by Rabbi Maurice Davis, now of White Plains, for $50,000, "which he paid back over the course of several years."

The rabbi, ironically, has since become prominent in organizing families to fight religious cults. "Jones's name kept cropping up in the work I do in deprogramming," Rabbi Davis said, "but there was no indication of his organizing such a cult in Indianapolis."

Mr. Jones, in his People's Temple, found transients and set up a soup kitchen. He visited a congregant in a badly run nursing home, "carried her out in a blanket," according to Mr. Hunter, and started his own nursing homes.

"They were crowded, but clean and humane, and for a while they were among the best in the city," the executive director said. "Soon he began to demand sacrifices — members of his church gave more liberally of their time and money than those of other churches."

Mr. Jones had what Mr. Hunter calls a "very positive personality" and seemed to be able to raise money easily. "He once said, 'Everything I touch turns to money. I'd have been a millionaire if I had not been called this way,' " Mr. Hunter said.

FRANK JOHNSTON/THE WASHINGTON POST/GETTY IMAGES

A child lay between a Jonestown, Guyana, couple as they and other People's Temple members linked arms before dying

'MORE COMMITTED THAN SOME'

Mr. Jones was named head of the Indianapolis human-rights organization, Mr. Hunter recalled, and "he was seen by many as a person much more heavily committed to social concerns than the average, but a person with driving desire."

Rabbi Davis recalls Mr. Jones as being primarily involved in interracial matters. "He had an interracial family," he said. "He was part Indian, his wife was white, they adopted children of different races" — one was black and one was Korean — "and finally, in about 1964, he left Indiana, saying it was too racist for him."

Mr. Hunter recalled that, too, and more: "Jim had also become interested in the atomic bomb, Vietnam, and other matters. He had left for a while to teach at the University of Hawaii and he spent two years in Brazil organizing orphanages and a mission.

DAVID HUME KENNERLY/GETTY IMAGES

The Reverend Jim Jones's bloated body, far right, sewn together after a hasty autopsy, lies on the ground along with the bodies of his followers.

The Indianapolis church was disbanded after Mr. Jones and his followers left for California. "We visited them there once," Mr. Hunter said. "He had built a church and included a swimming pool in the sanctuary. It was supposed to be for baptisms but he told the kids to use it after school."

DEMANDS FOR SOCIAL JUSTICE

Mr. Hunter, whose Fellowship of Reconciliation organized some of the first freedom rides in the South and spawned both the American Civil Liberties Union and the National Conference of Christians and Jews, said that Mr. Jones demanded much from his members in the fields of social and racial justice.

"He once told me he demanded that each member of the congregation write a letter about some social issue." Mr. Hunter recalled. The pastor had set up shelters for brutalized animals, initiated a job rehabilitation program and sent young people to college.

Mr. Hunter shook his head. “Jim had ambitions and he was autocratic. The idea of that community in Guyana was not evil, hacking out a community of love. But bodyguards to enforce love?”

Rabbi Davis said, “I keep thinking what happens when the power of love is twisted into the love of power.”

Then he recalled an incident in Indianapolis: “When he bought our temple we had an eternal light going. Jim asked us to leave it. He wanted to keep it burning as a sign of our friendship and what we stood for. All last night I kept wondering, where did it go out?”

Jones Used Bible-Thumping and Politics of Brotherhood

BY LACEY FOSBURGH | NOV. 23, 1978

SAN FRANCISCO, NOV. 22 — The middle-aged black woman always wore a plain dark suit and a small hat and she used to stand, day in and day out, month after month, on one of the main streets here soliciting funds for the People's Temple.

"It's for the Rev. Jim Jones," she would say to people as they stopped. "He tries to live what the Gospel preaches."

Or, she might say something just a little different. "It's for the Rev. Jim Jones. He's helping people become somebody."

In interviews during the last four days with a broad range of people, including a number of former devotees of the now deceased Mr. Jones, each person in turn has emphasized the same points to explain why people joined the sect.

MIXTURE OF RELIGION AND POLITICS

The key points seem to be some combination of religious and political motivation, as well as, on another level, a need for rehabilitation.

Members and former members of the group range from "the lowest economic group of blacks," as one reporter for the leading black newspaper here put it, to middle-class people of all races. There were one-time drug addicts, former convicts, former prostitutes, living in crowded quarters, sleeping on the floor in sleeping bags, alongside engineers, nurses, high school students, government workers and lawyers.

While virtually all sources agree that the membership of the church was 80 to 90 percent black, some people stress the troubled, needy aspect of the constituency: others, the humanitarian, idealistic, even political facet of Mr. Jones's appeal.

While this appeal was not strictly religious, the religious content of his message was fundamentalist, born-again Christianity. He quoted liberally and knowledgeably from the Bible and pictured Jesus as a social activist. Heaven, though, was the great reward.

From the pulpit he preached about brotherhood and equality and he called for integration. But he warned repeatedly and even with hysteria, people have said, that "a race war is coming."

Even as he would say, "Now let's all turn and hug the person standing next to you," he would warn of the killing and destruction that he said was ahead. What it was that drew people to his ranks seems to be a combination of attractions.

Today, for example, there is 76-year-old Francis E. Carter in Boise, Idaho, a retired agent for the Internal Revenue Service whose three children in turn joined the People's Temple when they all still lived in San Francisco and were quite young.

A year and a half ago they all moved to the Guyana headquarters with Mr. Jones.

CHILDREN GAVE UP DRUGS

Mr. Carter had watched, he said, as each of his children in high school became involved with drugs, began to drink and "care about nothing but rock music." But, then, he said, through involvement with the People's Temple, they gave up drugs, became "rehabilitated and got better." He always thought it was a good thing, he added. "They certainly improved."

He spoke as he waited for a telephone to ring, bringing word whether any of these children, or his three grandchildren, had survived the mass suicide in Guyana.

At almost the same time his eldest son, Tim, now 30, a Vietnam veteran who joined the People's Temple when he was 21, was arrested under still-undisclosed charges in Guyana.

"Do my children look unhappy?" he asked looking at photographs he had received of them from the compound in Jonestown. "No," he answered, but his brother William said he disagreed.

'BRAINWASHED LIKE MOONIES'

"I think the kids were brainwashed just like the Moonies," he said.

While a lot of so-called cults are known to attract young, middle-class white people who seemingly find purpose and identity through their involvement in the intense, autocratic regulation of their new life, the People's Temple also had another, entirely different, facet, people say.

Indeed not only was the group predominantly black, but it also had large numbers of middle-aged and even elderly members.

"All these old people felt they had become somebody through joining the Temple," said Tom Fleming, a reporter for San Francisco's leading black newspaper, The Sun Reporter, as well as a close friend of Mr. Jones.

'THEIR LIVES WERE BETTER'

"They weren't neglected anymore," he went on. "They now had everything from social organizations to preschool kid groups to be part of and they had a whole new life. I was amazed at their dedication. They had clearly found something. At least it gave them some home. Their lives were better."

"After all," he added, "they were from the lowest economic group of blacks. They were nobodies and now they were somebodies."

Fifty-year-old Al Mills has a different story to tell, of people with income and employment — or perhaps just a regular welfare or Social Security check — who joined the People's Temple out of a combination of political and religious motivation.

Significantly, however, with continued involvement, they gave up a way of life, quit their jobs, separated from their friends and even, in many cases, turned over an enormous amount of property to Mr. Jones.

POSSIBILITY OF SOCIALIST DEMOCRACY

In 1969 Mr. Mills was a laboratory technician for the Standard Oil Company of California as well as the social activist chairman of his

Disciples of Christ Church. He had had a long involvement in civil rights, marched in Selma, Ala., had been arrested for his political beliefs and he was originally attracted to the People's Temple because it believed in the possibilities of a socialist democracy.

That summer he took a tour organized by Mr. Jones up to the church's headquarters in Ukiah in Northern California. He was attracted immediately to the man because, he said, "He mixed fundamentalist Christianity with social activism."

"I was extremely impressed because Jones was very concerned about racial integration and civil rights."

He and his wife, Jeannie, attended the church service, and especially loved the choir, which sang protest songs rather than hymns. But Jeannie, for her part, was disturbed by something.

She was much more religious than her husband and she felt resentful when Mr. Jones would say that the Bible contradicted itself.

The couple returned home and Mrs. Mills immediately began to study the Bible and, to her amazement, she discovered that she agreed with Mr. Jones's analysis.

This was the turning point, Mr. Mills said here. Everything came together for them, and they decided to dedicate themselves to the communal, activist way of life Mr. Jones offered. They quit their jobs and moved north with five children.

FORCED TO CONFESS 'CRIMES'

In the next two years Mr. Mills turned over $50,000 worth of property, an automobile and $4,000 in cash. He had also been forced to sign pledges to commit suicide, and confessions to crimes he had not committed, and by 1972 he was totally disenchanted with the minister and left the church.

For Wanda Johnson, 42, it was much more difficult to leave and she is awaiting word whether her 12-year-old son is among the dead in the Guyana headquarters.

She originally met Mr. Jones when she attended adult education classes in Ukiah and he was teaching American history and comparative religion.

"At the time," she said, "I had a strong need for religious comfort in my life and he provided it." She attended Sunday services. "He had charisma. He had personal power. He seemed very benevolent and talked about equality for all people. He was extremely concerned about the needs of children and the elderly."

NEWSPAPER EDITOR REMEMBERS JONES

George Hunter, editor of The Ukiah Daily Journal, explained Mr. Jones's ability to draw people under his influence and gain control over them. He knew Mr. Jones both socially and professionally during the years the two lived in Ukiah.

"He was an extremely persuasive man who had a different faith and a different message for everyone he dealt with. He was able to hook in with each one in an individual way."

Mr. Jones was also very effective at getting his followers to believe that the measure of their devotion and loyalty had to be expressed financially. In the beginning, Wanda Johnson said, there was "no forced offering, you could give if you wanted."

THE SECT GOT 10 PERCENT

Then, she said, he imposed a rule "that you had to give over 10 percent of your earnings and assets."

"This was not for him, but for the church and the senior citizen's center and the school for retarded boys. It was for the good works."

"But," she went on, "he kept upping the ante and finally you had to give all. It was a question of, 'How devoted are you?' "

Within one year after she joined, she had given Mr. Jones her eight acres of property, her three-bedroom house, new four-wheel-drive pickup truck that was later shipped to Guyana, a 1965 Mustang, and $2,000 in savings.

In return, she was given a $2-a-week allowance.

Jim Jones — From Poverty to Power of Life and Death

BY ROBERT LINDSEY | NOV. 26, 1978

LOS ANGELES, NOV. 25 — He promised utopia and delivered death. And when warnings came of how it might end — and they came for more than year — almost no one listened.

The Rev. Jim Jones, who died with hundreds of his followers in Guyana last weekend, sprang out of dreary poverty in an industrial backwater of Indiana. At 16, he came under the influence of a woman at least four years older than he was who aroused his social conscience, and at 19, he began teaching a brand of Christian goodness as pure as that preached by Jesus himself in the Sermon on the Mount.

As he grew older, Mr. Jones fought racism, championed black causes, built nursing homes for the elderly, clothed the needy, rehabilitated drug addicts and prostitutes, became an early opponent of the Vietnam War, and campaigned for government aid to feed and house the poor.

But, according to interviews with friends, relatives, religious leaders and others who knew Jim Jones in the 47 years of a curious life, he was not always what he appeared to be.

He was a handsome, shy youth of 19 when he first mounted a pulpit. He became a faith healer who built a theocratic dictatorship that used religion to camouflage a bitter class hatred and fascination with Marxism that his wife said took root when he was a teen-ager.

ARRESTED FOR LEWD CONDUCT

Mr. Jones became a bisexual, according to several of his aides. He was arrested here for lewd conduct at a theater frequented by homosexuals. He demanded that scores of women in his church submit to him. From his pulpit, he ranted for hours on the evils of sexual temptation, but used his own charm, dark good looks and overt suggestions of sexuality to help maintain his spell over female followers.

He was a brilliant organizer and a spellbinding preacher who patterned his style after that of Father Divine, the vastly popular and successful black preacher of the 1930's through 1960's, many of whose followers considered him the personification of God.

He was a skilled manipulator of the political process whose style of mixing religion with social activism was so plausible that he was courted by political leaders and appointed to important government positions in Indianapolis and San Francisco.

And experts say he was, near the end of his life, almost certainly insane.

BORN IN RURAL INDIANA

James Warren Jones was born near Lynn, Ind., in a house that was little more than a shack, on May 13, 1931. The economy of the town of 1,350 people, 55 miles east of Indianapolis, was and is based on death. It has 13 businesses, five of them coffin makers. There's one blinking stoplight in the middle of town, one restaurant, a town hall and five churches.

His father, James T. Jones, who was 47 years old when his son was born, was one of 12 children in a poor farm family. He had been gassed in combat during World War I and was an invalid, frequently suffering painful emphysema-like attacks.

Years later. Mr. Jones would explain from the pulpit that he had compassion for blacks because he was the product of a biracial marriage, saying his father was part Cherokee Indian. But, like many stories he told, it apparently was not true. "There wasn't an ounce of Indian in our family," Barbara Shaffer, a cousin, said this week.

Mr. Jones's mother, Lynetta, was 17 years younger than his father and was described by people who knew her as a domineering woman who frequently derided her husband's inability to make a living, forcing her to find work in the factories and as a waitress. Almost daily, according to these accounts, she nagged her only child that he must make something of himself.

Mr. Jones would say later that he had been frequently and unmercifully beaten by his father, whom he portrayed as a Ku Klux Klan member with a strong hatred of blacks. He asserted that he was once beaten for bringing a black friend home to play, and he also said that once, when he brought a stray dog home, his father made him get rid of it and then beat him because there was no food for the animal.

At the age of 16, he took a full-time job working nights at Reid Memorial Hospital in Richmond, 13 miles north of Lynn, where he was attending Richmond High School. At the hospital, he met a nurse, Marceline Boswell, who was at least 20 — by some accounts she was 22 — and they became sweethearts.

His girlfriend was a slender, intelligent young woman who, for as long as anyone could remember, had a compassion for people with problems.

"Marceline was always for the underdog," her mother, Charlotte Baldwin, reminisced this week. "When she received her first paycheck from the hospital, she gave some to a local widow with 10 children." One of her two sisters, Eloise Clingman, added: "Marcie was one of a kind, always helping others."

'WE ALL CALLED HIM DOC'

At school, the youth was regarded as quiet, serious about getting good grades and intent on fulfilling his mother's desire that he go to college and make something of his life. His goal became a medical career.

"We all called him Doc," Gordon Samuels, a high school classmate, said. "He was very quiet, very reserved and not overly involved — nothing like the descriptions of the last few days. Back then, he just didn't seem to be that type of individual."

Another classmate, William Kehlenbrink, said: "We all thought he was going to be a doctor; he talked in medical terms all the time." Early in June 1919, Jones was graduated from Richmond High School. His yearbook noted, "Jim's six-syllable medical vocabulary astounds us all."

A few days later, on June 12, 1999, shortly after he had turned 18, Jim Jones married Marcie Boswell. In the earliest years of their marriage, friends said that she was much more self-confident and sure of herself, and they said her dedication to the underdog coalesced with his own feelings of compassion for blacks and the downtrodden.

JOINED FUNDAMENTALIST CHURCH

Mr. Jones enrolled at Indiana University in 1950 with plans to become doctor. His freshman roommate, Kenneth E. Lemons, now an Indianapolis accountant, recalled him this week as troubled and "maladjusted," frequently feeling compelled to check with his wife before making decisions. "She had become a mother figure to him," he said.

In Indianapolis, he joined a fundamentalist congregation and began serving as its occasional preacher, often espousing the cause of the poor and attacking the Establishment for ignoring the plight of blacks and other poor people. After a while, his career plans started to change. He dropped his goal to become a doctor, deciding instead to be a faith healer.

Years later, in a 1977 interview with The New York Times, his wife said that her husband had not been lured to the ministry by deep religious faith, but because it served his goal of achieving social change through Marxism.

When he was 18, she said, he told her his hero was Mao Tse-tung, who had just overthrown the Chinese Nationalist Government. And at 21, she said, he decided that the way to achieve social change was to mobilize people through religion.

"Jim used religion to try to get some people out of the opiate of religion," she said, adding that he had once slammed a Bible on a table and said, "I've got to destroy this paper idol!" If that was how he felt from the start, it was not what he told his congregation.

COLLEGE AMID POVERTY

In 1951, he enrolled in Butler University near Indianapolis, while he continued to serve as pastor of the church. But the couple had little money to support themselves, and it would be 10 years of off-and-on classes before he earned a degree. Meanwhile, his parents had separated and his father died in 1951, alone in a hotel, after suffering an attack from his war injuries.

In 1953, declaring that he was outraged at what he perceived as racial discrimination in his white congregation, Mr. Jones established his own church and pointedly opened it to all ethnic groups. To raise money, he imported monkeys and sold them door to door as pets.

LIKED CHURCH'S AUTONOMY

In the late 1950's, he gravitated to the Christian Church (Disciples of Christ), a middle-of-the-road Protestant denomination. In 1960, that church listed the People's Temple in Indianapolis as a branch. In its subsequent moves to California and then to Guyana, the People's Temple maintained the affiliation.

The church gives each congregation substantial autonomy, is considered liberal on social issues and permits each congregation to select its own pastor and nominate him for ordination — all features that attracted Mr. Jones. He was ordained in the church in February 1964, three years after obtaining a degree in secondary education from Butler. He had then served as pastor of the People's Temple for more than a decade.

He remained in Indianapolis until 1965, and for the most part, was in the mainstream of clerical and civic life, although his emphasis on helping the poor, especially blacks, made him conspicuous.

Several other changes occurred in Mr. Jones during these years: He began to claim that he could perform miracles, he demonstrated a remarkable skill for organizing projects, he realized the political value of a large religious congregation and he began to enjoy power.

A turning point had come in the early 1950's. After attending a service in Philadelphia conducted by Father Divine, he told friends how impressed he had been and said that he was determined to change his own style. Ross E. Case, one of his aides, recalled this week:

"He was always talking about sex, or Father Divine, or Daddy Grace, and was envious of how they were adored by their people and the absolute loyalty they got. Jim wanted all that affection and loyalty for himself."

During his dozen years in Indianapolis, he had started to urge his parishioners to call him "Father," and to address his wife as "Mother."

Aides later said that he began to fake healings during this period, using cooperative church members to claim that he had miraculously cured them, or using the intestines of animals as evidence to show that he had exorcised cancer from congregants. At the same time, there were some followers who alleged that he had actually cured them of arthritis or other ailments.

His wife worked closely with him as his church grew. They began to help poor blacks as well as whites, opening soup kitchens, helping poor people get jobs and establishing facilities for the elderly. In 1961, the couple had a son and named him Stephan Gandhi Jones.

BUILDING POLITICAL POWER

As his congregation grew, Mr. Jones realized that he could persuade its members to vote as a bloc on the social issues that interested him, and political leaders noticed his ability to assemble large numbers of people at campaign rallies.

In 1961, he applied for the job of Indianapolis Human Relations Commissioner and got it. "The selection committee thought," recalled Mayor Charles Boswell, "that being a pastor, he could pacify businesses that were discriminating in a calm and unemotional way. And in fact, he did."

The same year, the couple adopted a black child and named him James Jones Jr. Eventually they would adopt six other black, white and Korean children.

In the meantime, rumors were circulating in the church that Mrs. Jones was unhappy that her husband had been having affairs with members of his congregation, beginning in the early 1960's.

PREFERRED YOUNGER WOMEN

He told one friend that he felt "dirty" after having sexual intercourse with his wife and had a sense of guilt about it. He confided to another friend that he preferred sex with younger women, whom he was able to dominate more easily than his wife.

The minister's claims of faith healing and his mimicking of Father Divine, while successful in increasing the size of his congregation, made some church officials uneasy, but no efforts were made to discipline him.

One church official told Mr. Jones that he wanted to verify his claims of faith healing and said he would make an investigation, but Jones refused to cooperate and made plans to leave Indianapolis.

In the mid-1960's, old friends said they noticed a change in Mr. Jones, especially a growing sense of self-importance and autocratic methods in dealing with his flock, and he became impatient with criticisms, establishing an "interrogation committee" to challenge congregation members who disagreed with him.

Meanwhile, public officials in Indianapolis began investigating a large number of real-estate transfers from members of his church to Mr. Jones and to a profit-making corporation controlled by him, his wife and his mother.

Barton Hunter, who was a supervising official of the church in Indianapolis then, said that reports of those transactions were made to him and he questioned Mr. Jones about them. But he was satisfied that the minister was not taking the property for personal gain.

"There was evidence that he did have properties transferred to himself rather than the church," Mr. Hunter said, "but from his point of view, he was the church. As he saw it, he was able to handle the funds better than the church; he saw himself as the official embodiment of the church."

Mr. Jones had by now become highly effective preacher, Mr. Hunter said. "His style was a little like Billy Graham. He would say, 'The Bible says ... this is the way it is ....' It had great appeal with unsophisticated, and some sophisticated, people. In today's world, a lot of people like to hear 'this is the way, I know where I'm going, I invite you to go with me.' "

SAFE HAVEN IN CALIFORNIA

In 1965, Mr. Jones announced to his congregation that the world would be engulfed by a devastating thermonuclear war on July 15, 1967, and that it was therefore necessary to move to safe haven in northern California. He led about 70 families to Redwood Valley near Ukiah, a rural town set in the redwoods of Mendocino County, one of the places scouted by Mr. Case.

About half of these colonizers were black, and their arrival shocked some townspeople, but members of the group kept to themselves and were eventually considered good neighbors who worked hard and did not bother other people.

California has long had a reputation as a fertile ground for persuasive authority figures/religious leaders who offered easy answers to complex problems and offered to make decisions for their followers.

Dr. Louis J. West, chairman of the Department of Psychiatry at the University of California at Los Angeles, explained: "They expect California to be a utopia. But some get disillusioned when they get here, and they get mixed up with cults because they promise them the ties they are seeking. To lots of these people the cults look like utopia."

His intelligence, soft-spoken friendliness and seemingly earnest search for a better world impressed people in the conservative California town. In 1966, he was appointed chairman of the county grand jury. Robert Winslow, the judge who made the appointment, recalled:

"He was a very bright, humanistic person. He didn't seem to be a socialist. They were nice, concerned people. Their most significant characteristic was that they wanted to come to the aid of anyone in trouble. Jones wasn't a fanatic when I knew him, although people were emotionally dependent upon him. The people in his community built their entire lives around Jones and his church."

Although he was accepted socially and in the political establishment, few people attended his church. Then in October 1968, Timothy Stoen, a politically liberal Stanford University Law School graduate and a deputy district attorney, began to attend his services, largely, he said later, because of the emphasis on helping the poor.

The next year, he sold almost everything he owned to become a church member and an aide to Mr. Jones. He was, he said, influenced by the assassination of Dr. Martin Luther King, Jr.

Thomas E. Martin, the Mendocino County probation officer, said that Mr. Stoen's enrollment was a turning point. "He was highly respected in the community," Mr. Martin said, "and this gave the church instant credence."

'HE WORKED VERY HARD'

In 1970 the minister told Mr. Stoen that he believed he had a message that should be heard beyond Redwood Valley and he began preaching in low-income black neighborhoods in San Francisco. In 1971 he bought a church in San Francisco, calling it the People's Temple, and later another church in Los Angeles. Along the way, his brand of social and political revivalism caught the attention of California's liberal and radical political leaders.

"He bought 13 Greyhound-type buses," Mr. Stoen recalled. "He displayed the most brilliant organizational genius I have ever encountered. He could put 13 buses together for a trip in a day — that's how gifted he was and he worked very, very hard."

At its peak in the early 1970's, the church claimed a membership of almost 20,000, all in California.

Nonetheless, some church members began to complain privately to each other of Mr. Jones's marathon sermons, often lasting six hours or more, his preoccupation with sex, his emphasis on work that consumed almost all their spare time, and of rumors that more and more members were being forced to empty their bank accounts and sell their homes to raise money for the church.

But, Mr. Stoen said, Mr. Jones maintained discipline by keeping the members so tired that they had little time to complain, and by what he called "catharsis sessions," in which dissidents were ridiculed and beaten with paddies. In 1973, Mr. Stoen said that Mr. Jones seemed to be growing increasingly paranoid, interpreting any criticism as a deep personal affront. Others said he was changing in other ways.

BECAME JEKYLL AND HYDE

"I loved him," said Fannie Mobley, a black woman who was a church member from 1972 until 1976. "The way he sang, in such a beautiful voice, 'It Ain't Necessarily So' was lovely. But he changed; he turned from a beautiful Christian man to a Jekyll and Hyde monster."

"He started searching everybody who came in and he had people standing around with clubs," she said. On Thursday nights, church members were always shown a movie depicting Nazi atrocities against Jews, and Mr. Jones said that the United States Government was preparing crematoriums for blacks.

"He said the C.I.A. was out to get us; he didn't like the United States," Mrs. Mobley related. "He told us to believe in Marxism. He hated everybody, the President, but he said he liked Hitler and Lenin. He just went crazy, crazy.

"Oh, and he would talk for hours about sex, about how good he was and how women should think he was making love to them, not their husbands, and about how all the women sent him notes that they wanted to see him.

"He told everybody not to have sex until they got to the Promised Land, but when women told him they had no way to raise any money for him, he told them to go out on the streets. He said: 'You're good-looking, you ought to be able to get some money.' He was good-looking man, and he knew all the women liked his looks, and he'd use it, come up to you and say, 'Hello love, hello pet.' "

HOMOSEXUALITY AND SADISM

Wayne Pietila, a former bodyguard for Mr. Jones, said that the minister "had a voracious appetite for both men and women," and that he appointed one of his secretaries to arrange for women church members to sleep with him. Later, he said, some of these women complained that Jones was a sadistic lover.

Mr. Jones's wife, Mr. Pietila added, knew of these liaisons and seemed distraught about them, and on several occasions seemed to be close to a breakdown.

On Dec. 13, 1973, Mr. Jones was arrested in a Hollywood theater on lewd-conduct charge, after an undercover Los Angeles policeman said that Mr. Jones had tried to molest him. The charge was subsequently dismissed by the city attorney's office because of a dispute over the legality of the arrest. The arrest was not reported at the time, but was confirmed by law-enforcement sources here this week.

The same month that he was arrested, Mr. Jones dispatched a small party of church members to Guyana to scout locations for an agricultural commune. Meanwhile, he had begun a program to manipulate both the press and the political system.

CHAMPION OF FREE PRESS

He decided that the news media's most popular issue was freedom of the press and began deploring any potential infringement of it. For example, when four reporters in Fresno, Calif., were jailed because they refused to reveal their sources, Mr. Jones led group of members to Fresno to protest. He donated thousands of dollars to journalism organizations, advocated resistance to Government infringements on the press, and bombarded editors with letters.

Although an occasional negative article about the People's Temple appeared in newspapers, the ploy largely worked. He was even more successful with politicians.

"Jones could deliver 2,000 bodies on six hours' notice, and the politicians knew that," Mr. Stoen said. This, plus his apparently liberal views, made him popular with political leaders in' the city and state and even some at the national level.

"There was a time when, if you were running for office in San Francisco, and you counted in your votes the poor, the blacks, or young people, you'd better have Jones's support," recalled Corey Buscher, a former press secretary to San Francisco's Mayor, George Moscone. Mr. Moscone, one of the most visible politicians to court Mr. Jones, appointed him to the city Housing Authority in 1976, and he eventually became its chairman.

As his political power grew, so did the wealth of his church, which was collected by members in a variety of business enterprises and through levies of 25 to 40 percent of their gross incomes and sales of their homes and other property — many times against their will. They did so out of fear, they would later say.

$5 MILLION IN FOREIGN BANKS

Mr. Stoen said that he personally arranged for $5 million to be deposited in foreign banks, and he said the church's total assets were probably far greater.

In August 1977, New West magazine carried the first detailed critical report on his church, and Mr. Stoen recalled: "He had been paranoid before that, but after the New West article, he really became paranoid."

UTOPIA IN SOUTH AMERICA

Even before the article was printed, Mr. Jones had moved ahead with plans to relocate his congregation in Guyana, which he said would be a socialist utopia where all races could mix in peace and work for the common good. After he arrived in Guyana, he increasingly preached about dark forces that were out to shut down his experiment in communal living.

When the minister left San Francisco, he left behind an "administrative department," to which he spoke nightly via short-wave radio, and in code, to deal with "traitors." Defectors were bombarded with threats of beatings and killings, and at least one member, Christopher Lewis, was murdered in San Francisco in December 1977, although the police never established that the crime was connected with Mr. Jones. Still, Mr. Lewis's death was constantly cited by the administrative department — a kind of enforcement squad — to dissident members as a warning to keep quiet. Mr. Stoen said that Mr. Jones took any critical comment about the commune as a personal attack and said that anyone who left the church deserved to die.

Warnings to officials that something was seriously wrong in Guyana began in the summer of 1977. Mrs. Mobley said that she made 100 copies of the 1977 New York Times interview in which Mrs. Jones admitted her husband's longtime contempt for religion and his affection for Marxism and sent them to every politician whose name she could find, beginning with President Carter.

"I warned them that something like this was going to happen," she said in an interview, as she broke into tears.

"But nobody would listen."

CHRONOLOGY OF DESPERATE WARNINGS

More precise warnings and signals from Jones himself on what was about to happen began to come last spring:

April 10 — Relatives of the church members living in Guyana issued a statement accusing Mr. Jones of "human rights violations" and quoted him as having told a member: "I can say without hesitation that we are devoted to a decision that it is better even to die than to be constantly harassed from one continent to the next."

April 18 — Mr. Jones replied, confirming the possibility of mass suicide, writing in part: "Dr. Martin Luther King reaffirmed the validity of ultimate commitment when he told his Freedom Riders: 'We must develop the courage of dying for a cause.' We likewise affirm that before we will submit quietly to the interminable plotting and persecution of this politically motivated conspiracy, we will resist actively, putting our lives on the line if it comes to that.... We chose as our motto, not like those who march submissively into gas ovens, but like the valiant heroes who resisted in the Warsaw ghetto."

June 15 — Deborah Layton Blakely, after leaving the commune in May, said in an affidavit and in newspaper interviews that Mr. Jones was "obsessed with his place in history" and had paranoia of "maniacal" proportions. She told of rehearsals for mass suicide. She said that Mr. Jones had said that the purpose of the suicides was to "create an international incident" and that commune members were so broken by the fear of the minister and by exhaustion that they could not escape and might follow his orders to kill themselves.

June 22 — A former member, James Cobb, charged in a lawsuit filed against Mr. Jones in San Francisco that Mr. Jones was planning "mass murder" that "would result in the death of minor children not old enough to make voluntary and informed decisions about serious matters of any nature, much less insane proposals of collective suicide."

STATE DEPARTMENT FOUND NO BASIS

Meanwhile, many former members of the group sought help from the State Department, which responded that it had investigated the charges and found no basis for action, and a few newspapers began looking into the allegations.

Relatives of church members in Guyana at last prevailed on a San Francisco Bay area Congressman, Leo J. Ryan, to investigate the charges, and it was his visit that precipitated the mass suicide.

In his final days, there were reports that Mr. Jones, more than ever, harangued against the forces that were out to get him, against heterosexual relations between church members, and, according to a church

DON HOGAN CHARLES/NEW YORK TIMES CO./GETTY IMAGES

The Rev. Jim Jones in a family portrait made in Ukiah, Calif., in 1976, with wife, Marceline, at center, adopted children and sister-in-law with three children.

member who visited the commune in September, he repeatedly accused the male defectors from the church of being homosexuals.

His wife, Marcie, was near his side when Jones died. Witnesses said that his last words were: "Mother ... Mother ... ."

Mrs. Baldwin, Marceline Jones's mother, visited the commune in Guyana for three weeks and left only a few days before the Ryan party arrived.

In a curious interview that she gave to an Indiana newspaper after the mass suicide and killings, she said she still believed that her daughter and son-in-law had done good works and respected the commune in Guyana. Her daughter's last words to her were, "I have lived, not just existed."

The bodies of Jim and Marceline Jones were on their way home today, to be buried in Richmond, Ind.

Jones and 3 in Family Are to Be Buried at Sea

SPECIAL TO THE NEW YORK TIMES | NOV. 27, 1978

RICHMOND, IND., NOV. 26 — The remains of the Rev. Jim Jones, his wife and at least two of their children will be buried at sea after cremation at Dover, Del., in accordance with the wishes of his wife's family.

In a statement issued today on behalf of Mr. and Mrs. Walter Baldwin, the parents of Mr. Jones's wife, a funeral director here said: "After much consideration, the family of Marceline Baldwin Jones decided not to have Marceline, Reverend Jones and their children returned to Richmond for burial."

The director, Ernest W. Mills, owner of the Doan & Mills Funeral Home here, continued, "It is only natural that Mr. and Mrs. Baldwin wanted their daughter's body returned here for burial, and for this reason the original plans were made." Burial had originally been planned at Earlhaai Cemetery here.

CHAPTER 3

David Koresh: The Branch Davidians

Born to a 14-year-old mother, David Koresh was a lonely child and a high school dropout. When Koresh was 24, he joined a religious sect called the Branch Davidians. Over time he assumed control of the group, claiming to be a prophet. Koresh took a 14-year-old wife and fathered children with her and several other women in the group. Charges of child sexual and physical abuse led federal authorities to raid the armed group's compound in Waco, Tex., in 1993. After a 51-day siege, 79 Davidians, including Koresh, were killed in the blaze started by the authorities' attempt to force them from the building.

Bloody Sunday's Roots in Deep Religious Soil

BY PETER APPLEBOME | MARCH 2, 1993

WACO, TEX., MARCH 1 — Like a vein of ore in solid rock, religion runs through the heart of this city, which is sometimes known as Jerusalem on the Brazos River.

But in this city of 100,000 people, where almost everyone belongs to one of some 200 churches, the sect at the Mount Carmel compound 10 miles east of town lived in a world so insular that most people never knew it existed until Sunday's bloody shootout.

"These people were isolationists," said Derek Davis, a professor of church-state studies at Baylor University here. "The Davidians, as far as I know, have had no community involvement whatsoever. They're strictly isolated out there and serve no one except themselves."

Still, the cult strikes some as more a mutant gene than a total aberration — a group that tapped into the deep religious roots here and sprouted into something dark and twisted.

PEACEFUL ROOTS IN 1930'S

In fact, some familiar with the group, whose roots here go back to the 1930's, remember it from its early days as a slightly eccentric but unremarkable religious sect.

Harold Braun, who lives in nearby Otto, said that during the 1950's he used to deliver coastal Bermuda hay to the compound, whose residents he likened "Tennessee hillbillies who just wanted to be left alone." But he and others said the group has apparently become much more isolated in recent years.

Jack Stewart, president of the Greater Waco Chamber of Commerce, said: "The sad part about this group is that it has evolved from the peaceful, pastoral group that it started as in the 1930's. Only since this most recent leader have they begun to acquire some of the weaponry and attitudes that they have."

Calvin Ross of Lone Star Music and Sound Company remembers the group's leader, who was then known as Vernon Howell but who later changed his name to David Koresh. Mr. Ross described him as an odd mix of religious zealot and frustrated rock performer, who often came to his shop looking for guitars and invariably tried to drive as hard a bargain as possible.

BOUGHT 4 RIFLES

"He was a frustrated rock musician who wanted to be a rock star, gave up on that dream and then wanted to be Jesus Christ," he said. "He had a kind of arrogant air about him."

Leo Bradshaw, owner of a gun shop where Mr. Howell and other sect members sometimes bought weapons said he had sold four Ruger

Mini-14 assault rifles to the group a few years ago but does not know where the group acquired its arsenal.

"If they have been buying it locally, they've been buying it very discreetly," he said.

CONTACTS WERE LIMITED

Mr. Bradshaw said almost everything the group did locally was discrete. Some members may have worked in town, but they apparently grew much of their own food, raised Holstein and Jersey cows for milk and lived in something close to a self-sufficient fashion.

When asked where they shopped, Mr. Bradshaw said: "They don't. The Amish are very stylish compared to these women. I imagine they make most of their own clothes."

Even many of those who live near the group's compound, which is the size of a city block and sits on 77 acres 10 miles east of town, said they knew next to nothing about the group and its practices.

"They never really bothered anybody," said Richard Cornelius. "Nobody even knew they were around."

The Davidians most public moment in recent years turned out to be an ominously prophetic one.

UNSWERVING ALLEGIANCE

Two competing sects, one led by Mr. Koresh, the other led by a rival leader, George Roden, found themselves in a shootout on Nov. 3, 1987. As a result Mr. Koresh and his followers were charged with attempted murder.

Mr. Koresh's followers clogged the third floor of the McLennan County Courthouse, the women dressed in long dresses with blouses buttoned up to their necks, with babies clinging tightly to them.

According to an account in The Waco Tribune-Herald, the extent of their allegiance to Mr. Koresh was clear and chilling.

Before the trial, visiting Judge Herman Fitts asked if there were any witnesses in the courtroom who needed to be sworn in. No one rose. Mr. Koresh's lawyer, Gary Coker, repeated the same request. Again no one rose. Mr. Koresh then stood with a smile and said: "It's all right. You've done nothing wrong. Stand." Only then did his followers stand to be sworn in.

The case against him ended in mistrial, and the charges were later dropped.

Those who did come in contact with the group often came away with reason to be concerned.

'MADMAN LIVING IN WACO'

When Mr. Koresh made a demonstration tape at a local recording studio, he provided his own preview of things to come.

"There's a madman living in Waco," one song went. "Pray to the Prince of Hell."

To some, one glaring unanswered question is why it took so long for action to be taken against the group. Even if its public profile was low, some former members and relatives of members say, authorities knew enough that they should have taken action sooner.

David Slawson, a 41-year-old carpenter in Idaho, said he had watched events unfold in Waco with a sense of anger, helplessness and frustration.

"What happened didn't have to happen," he said. "We had enough information to put them away 10 years ago."

Mr. Slawson said he had lived in the community in the late 1960's and feared two nieces were there now. He added that he and his sister had repeatedly tried to alert authorities about the group, expressing concerns to the police, children's protective services, a county judge and school officials.

"Vernon Howell reminds me more and more of Jim Jones and Manson," he said. "It's mind boggling. We are really angry. People are dying. There was no need for this."

Bob Boyd, program director for Children's Protective Services, a division of the Texas Department of Protective and Regulatory

Services, the agency with jurisdiction over allegations of child abuse and neglect, said confidentiality laws forbid him from commenting on the children now in custody and on complaints the agency may have received.

Exactly what was reported and to whom is not certain.

But Professor Davis of Baylor said the more unusual aspects of the group's religion would have been tolerated in a community familiar with and tolerant of a wide range of Christian expression.

"For the most part, even the legal authorities have stayed away, and I really think it's out of this tradition of respect for religious liberty," he said. "Of course, this is a tradition that's part of the American tradition, but I think it's particularly strong here, because we do have such a diversity of faith here. People have respected their right to be there. But they also feel their right to practice their faith does not put them above the law."

'Messiah' Fond of Bible, Rock and Women

BY SAM HOWE VERHOVEK | MARCH 3, 1993

WACO, TEX., MARCH 2 — Years before he began ordering the Branch Davidians to arm themselves for the apocalypse, before he told them he was Jesus Christ, David Koresh built up his following in a far more ordinary way: by playing rock music with them, sharing an occasional beer, and, most of all, by preaching Scripture with unwavering conviction.

Even some sect members who came to conclude that he was dangerously unstable, and who managed to shake free of his cult, described him as having first lured them with his fondness for good times and a gentle promise of truth.

"He had this amazing ability to recite verse," said Robyn Bunds, now 23, who joined the sect in California and later became one of at least 19 "wives" of Mr. Koresh and mother of one of his many children. "He just has a good way of interpreting the Scriptures. He is very believable."

After a deadly shootout with law-enforcement officials on Sunday, Mr. Koresh had still not turned himself in today as a standoff dragged on into the night at the cult's fortified compound 10 miles from here. Earlier in the day he had said that he and his followers would surrender if a rambling discourse on the Bible was broadcast over the radio.

Mr. Koresh found the people whom he ultimately brought here, and who engaged in the shootout that left four Federal agents and at least two cult members dead, in California, Australia and Britain, and in at least three Texas towns. His followers were people who had lost jobs, lovers or simply a sense of belonging to the world in which they lived.

RECRUITED IN SUPERMARKET

And though some began to question his increasingly self-centered depictions of religious truth, many of those who remained were willing to believe that they were indeed living with the Messiah and had to do whatever he said.

"They believe so much in who they think he is that his more fanatical followers might shoot anyone who tried to stand up to Vernon," said Marc Breault, a former member from Melbourne, Australia, whose trail to Mr. Koresh's compound started when he was recruited in a supermarket in Riverside, Calif.

In calling him Vernon, Mr. Breault was referring to Mr. Koresh's birth name, Vernon Wayne Howell. It was legally changed to David Koresh in 1990; California court documents show that the cult leader requested the new name "for publicity and business purposes," while Mr. Koresh told Branch Davidians that he did it to reflect his conviction that he is the head of the Biblical House of David. Koresh is a Hebrew transliteration of Cyrus, the name of the Persian emperor who allowed the Jews held captive in Babylon to return to Israel.

More recently, the 33-year-old Mr. Koresh has simply said that he is the Messiah. "If the Bible is true, then I'm Christ," he said on an audio tape for his followers that was quoted in the Waco Tribune-Herald and whose contents were also confirmed by the relative of a former cult member.

MEMORIZING THE BIBLE

Vernon Howell, born in Houston in 1959 to a single mother, has a history of learning disabilities and a string of incomplete attendance records at schools in the Dallas area. He dropped out of high school in Garland, a Dallas suburb, in 1977; the only record of any extracurricular activity was one quarter in the high school band, said Steve Knagg, a spokesman for the Garland Independent School District.

But despite his unspectacular performance in school, the future Mr. Koresh did exhibit one striking trait from an early age: an ability to memorize passages of the Bible, and to string them together to make just about any point he wished to. He attended services of the Seventh-Day Adventist Church and he spent a lot of time in prayer.

"He would come home and go to the barn and pray for hours," his mother, Bonnie Haldeman, told The Associated Press on Monday from her home in the East Texas town of Chandler. Neighbors said Mrs. Haldeman left for Waco this morning, and she could not be found here today.

Sometime in the late 1970's, Mr. Koresh drifted to Southern California. By most accounts from cult members he seems to have spent most of his time proselytizing on behalf of the Branch Davidians, a renegade offshoot of the Seventh-Day Adventists, and demonstrating his prowess on the guitar.

With wavy hair, soft eyes behind wire-frame glasses and a boyish grin, Mr. Koresh also proved himself attractive to the women who congregated at a five-bedroom sect house in La Verne, a community about 30 miles east of Los Angeles. Whatever his religious convictions, they did not preclude him from having sex with the women, even after he married a 14-year-old girl, Rachel Jones, in 1984. She was the daughter of a Branch Davidian follower.

TEXAS TRANSFORMATION

It was not until 1986 or 1987, when Mr. Koresh moved with many of his followers to what had been a quiet, pastoral retreat of the Branch Davidians here, that Mr. Koresh began transforming himself into a self-proclaimed Messiah, former cult members said. It was also in Texas that he began developing the conviction that his followers should prepare for a bloody confrontation with nonbelievers that would end in his resurrection — and their ticket to Heaven.

The followers were instructed to buy guns, which they did at gun stores in the Waco area and by mail order. Mr. Koresh himself bought six pistols at a gun show in Houston last year when he went to visit his grandmother, Jean Holub.

"He did say, 'Grandma, it's coming a time, I'm going to bring you a little gun,' " a tearful Mrs. Holub said today in an interview at her home in a middle-class Houston neighborhood. "He said, 'It's coming a time we won't be in our homes, they'll be breaking in on us and we've got to protect our families.' "

ELIZABETH BARANYAI/SYGMA/GETTY IMAGES

David Koresh, then known as Vernon Howell, his wife Rachel and their son Cyrus in front of their house in 1986.

He took control of the compound after a long struggle with other aspiring leaders that included a 1987 gun battle pitting Mr. Koresh and seven of his followers against George Roden, one of his rivals. A jury acquitted all of the followers of attempted murder, Mr. Koresh's trial ended in a hung jury and charges were dropped, and Mr. Roden was later confined to a mental hospital after being found not guilty by reason of insanity in the killing of an Odessa, Tex., man.

Though he seems to have forbidden some of the women from leaving the compound at all, Mr. Koresh relied on wages from the jobs of other members to finance his occasional trips outside the Waco area, including one to Israel, one to Britain, and at least two to Australia.

None of the cult members or their relatives interviewed could trace a specific moment when Mr. Koresh began casting himself as a prophet who could foretell the bloody but glorious ending in store for his followers. But he did tell the women, including the wives of some cult members, that it was God's will that he have sex with them and create the children who could help rule a future House of David.

"Only the Lamb is to be given the job to raise up the seed of the House of David, isn't he?" he says on the audio tape to his followers provided to the local newspaper here. "Remember Mary and God. Yeah?"

Among the former cult members, opinions simply vary about whether Mr. Koresh is actually willing to carry out his visions of a violent, martyred end to his life. He has repeatedly complained since the shootout about bleeding from the stomach. But because he has also kept up a fairly regular stream of talk for more than 56 hours, there is reason to doubt that he is seriously injured.

Mr. Breault told The Waco Tribune-Herald that he believed Mr. Koresh might be going through a typical "bit of theatrics" with his complaint.

"Vernon was always saying he was sick and near death," said Mr. Breault. "He's real big on stomach sickness. He always complained about his stomach, saying he was in pain because of the people's sins."

With Plenty of Food, Water and Bibles, Texas Cult Can Hold Out for a While

BY SAM HOWE VERHOVEK | MARCH 5, 1993

THEY BOUGHT HUNDREDS of 40- and 50-pound sacks of grain, mostly rice and millet, at two food co-ops near Dallas. A neighbor saw them in recent months spend nearly $6,000 on canned goods and juices at Sam's Club, a discount warehouse on the outskirts of Waco.

There is a water tower in the inner courtyard of their fortified compound, along with a dirty but usable well. Although agents for the Federal Bureau of Investigation have yet to cut off electricity to the compound, there are at least two generators and a stockpile of batteries available if they do.

And there are plenty of each of the two things that the Branch Davidians' self-proclaimed Messiah, David Koresh, tells cult members to use most of the day: Bibles for study and shovels for work on a network of tunnels and bunkers.

ENOUGH SUPPLIES FOR WEEKS

Four days after Mr. Koresh's followers engaged Federal agents in a deadly gun battle at the compound 10 miles northeast of Waco, the F.B.I. agent in charge of getting them to come out conceded today that cult members seemed to have settled into "their normal routine."

And accounts from former cult members, Federal officials and a neighbor who watched the stockpiles accumulate all suggest that there are enough supplies inside to allow the nearly 100 people there to survive for weeks and possibly for months.

Even as hundreds of law-enforcement officials with tanks and weaponry keep the 77-acre property surrounded, the F.B.I. agent, Jeffrey Jamar, says that there are no plans to storm the compound and that he wants a peaceful resolution to the standoff.

That is what Mr. Koresh says, too, but he insists that the only one who can tell him just when to come out is God.

Hours after the gun battle, the cult leader told CNN that he had been "shot through the guts" and was lying on a sheet soaked with his own blood. But he has been talking away since then, sometimes quoting from the Bible for hours during telephone conversations with negotiators. "He seems to have recovered miraculously," Mr. Jamar said dryly at a news briefing today.

The authorities have refused to let any of the 20 children or three adults who have left the compound talk to reporters. But a picture of what life is like there now can be assembled from brief reports provided by officials who have talked to them, and from interviews with two former cult members who say that Mr. Koresh frequently talked about a day when heathens would lay siege to the compound and how his followers would respond.

'STARVED THE PEOPLE'

Even as he stockpiled large amounts of food, Mr. Koresh never let any of the cult members eat very much of it. Marc Breault, a computer programmer in Melbourne, Australia, who left the compound in 1989, said Mr. Koresh was obsessed with the notion of keeping a year's supply of food on hand and that he rationed it strictly.

"Vernon sort of starved the people," said Mr. Breault, referring to Mr. Koresh by his birth name, Vernon Howell, which the cult leader legally changed in 1990. "The idea was that we were being prepared for war, and with war comes famine. He said the rest of the people who were out there, the heathen, the ones who were used to eating whatever you wanted to eat when you wanted to eat it, they wouldn't be used to famine, so we would survive while they wouldn't."

Another former cult member, who spoke on condition of anonymity because of fears of reprisals by the cult, recalled that Mr. Koresh enforced his eating rules with a vengeance.

Once he caught one of his followers, whom he had sent into Waco on an errand, sneaking a hamburger at McDonald's. He flew into a blind rage, and called all of his followers into a meeting, the former member said.

"Why have you betrayed me?" a tearful Mr. Koresh asked his hungry follower.

Dan Hartnett, the associate director of the Federal Bureau of Alcohol, Tobacco and Firearms, said today that the routine followed by cult members included women working in the kitchen and many of the men "primarily involved in construction." Even as the siege continues and many cult members are busy serving as armed lookouts, the construction appears to be going on.

Both Federal and local officials have confirmed that there is a system of tunnels and bunkers underneath the compound, but they say they do not know how advanced it is. Lloyd Sandstrom, a school-bus driver who lives near the compound, said he had watched some of the construction from a nearby pasture.

"They have underground bunkers out there," he said in an interview today. "They built the last one over the last year and a half. It's too big for a root cellar. I estimate one side at 60 to 80 feet."

Mr. Sandstrom has also seen other evidence of the cult's self-sufficiency. "Regarding their ability to hold out, they have their own generators," he said. "I've seen them. They have their own water well. My neighbors and I have talked about how long they could last. I estimate they could withstand a standoff like this for three to four months, and my neighbors agree."

DESTROYING THE 'BABYLONIANS'

Military-style drills for both men and women, including chants, were part of the daily routine at the compound, and the two former members said they believed they were probably continuing.

Among Mr. Koresh's regular chants was a simple one he invented himself. Half the followers would shout out, "Who's gonna destroy the Babylonians?" then march in place for three counts before the other half would yell out in response, "We're gonna destroy the Babylonians!"

The authorities also said today that they had heard what appeared to be movie videotapes in the background during some of the negotiators' discussions with Mr. Koresh. No one could say what movies they were, but Mr. Breault said the cult leader had three definite favorites, all about the Vietnam War: "Platoon," "Full Metal Jacket" and "Hamburger Hill."

"He showed those just over and over and over again to us," recalled Mr. Breault. "He told us this was what we could look forward to. He would say the Bible prophesies war. We were being toughed. He wanted us to learn what it was like to be in a war."

The compound itself, painted in peach, consists of one large L-shaped building that contains dormitory-style residences, a gymnasium, a chapel and an adjacent four-story watchtower. Some, but not all of the walls, are fortified with cinderblocks, which are visible in aerial photographs.

Another report from Federal officials at the briefing today, that they could hear Mr. Koresh reading long passages from the Bible, apparently with some of his followers present, is consistent with what Mr. Breault termed his normal response whenever the cult leader was tense.

"When Vernon gets stressed out, what he does is give Bible sessions," he said. "It's mostly to reassure himself and to rev himself up." Asked if the cult leader had any favorite passages, Mr. Breault cited a passage from Psalm 38, a Psalm of David: "Mine enemies are lively, and they are strong; and they that hate me wrongfully are multiplied."

One issue that remains unclear is how scared, if at all, the cult members inside the compound are right now. Case workers for the Children's Protective Services here, a state agency, described the understandable fear among the children who witnessed the shootout and have been released. But the authorities have not commented on what they know about the adults who remain there.

"Some are real believers in Vernon and they'll do anything; it's O.K.," said a relative of a cult member. "Some people are just sick and tired; they've lost everything. They believe he's God, but they hate God; they think he's a real bastard, and all they can look forward to is dying and getting the pain out of the way. And a lot of people have just lost the capacity to really worry about it on their own. They're so mind-washed, they'll do whatever Vernon says."

Talks With Leader of Sect Have Stalled

BY PETER APPLEBOME | MARCH 8, 1993

WACO, TEX., MARCH 7 — A week after the bloody shootout at the Branch Davidian compound near here, negotiations are stalled, tempers are fraying and the authorities said they appeared to be going backward, not forward, in efforts to resolve their standoff with besieged cult members.

"I call them disappointing at this time," Bob A. Ricks, the spokesman here for the Federal Bureau of Investigation, said of negotiations with the cult's leader, David Koresh. "We are going through a very frustrating and disappointing period in the negotiation process."

He said that negotiators had failed to achieve the release of a young girl as expected today and that Mr. Koresh had become increasingly testy and subject to mood changes in telephone negotiations with law officers.

'STATE OF IRRITABILITY'

"What we are seeing more underlying the discussions is a state of irritability that seems to be existing, that pops up almost without notice," Mr. Ricks said. "Then he'll go back into a calm period of religious discussion. But we are seeing more of an irritability."

Notes of frustration and anger in his voice, Mr. Ricks stressed that the negotiations remain at the mercy of Mr. Koresh and that they could drag on indefinitely or end abruptly depending on the cult leader's mood.

"It could be resolved in the next hour," Mr. Ricks said this morning. "It's within his power."

Today marked a full week since last Sunday's 45-minute gun battle at the cult's 77-acre compound 10 miles east of here. The gun battle killed four agents with the Bureau of Alcohol, Tobacco and Firearms and at least three cult members.

Director Stephen E. Higgins of the firearms bureau, speaking on the CBS News program "Face the Nation," today denied reports that the bureau had gone ahead with the raid despite information that the cult might have been warned of the raid in advance.

"Our agents walked into an ambush," Mr. Higgins said. "We would not send our agents into a situation where we didn't think we had that element of surprise."

And he shed new light on just how much firepower the cult members had at their disposal. He said one of the bureau's agents saw the cult's armory before the Federal forces retreated last week.

"He said he'd never seen more arms in a room than he saw in that room that day," Mr. Higgins said.

At the compound there was no progress, just a wearying series of games of psychological cat and mouse between Mr. Koresh and the law officers surrounding the compound.

Mr. Ricks said a negotiating session Saturday night lasted until 3:15 A.M. and then picked up again this morning. Officers expected to obtain the release of a 6-year-old girl named Melissa but said Mr. Koresh abruptly changed his mind and the release fell through.

Later he rejected a delivery of milk for the children in the compound after earlier demanding it.

Thus far, 21 children and two women have been released from the compound. Law officers believe 17 children, 47 women and 43 men remain.

Instead of the release of the girl, law officers were treated to a serenade of rock music recorded by Mr. Koresh that blared out of speakers at the compound, apparently as a psychological salvo let loose by Mr. Koresh.

Mr. Ricks said in negotiations with Mr. Koresh, the cult leader alternated between religious discussions and practical arguments about how a release could be worked out. His main concern, Mr. Ricks said, seemed to be getting out his message on his own terms.

"David Koresh continues to express concern that he will be unable to tell his side of the story," Mr. Ricks said.

Mr. Ricks said Mr. Koresh continued to say he was waiting for a message from God before deciding to leave the compound. And he said that some members apparently want to leave but that a deal to let them go had fallen apart. He did not explain details of the rejected deal.

One added element of uncertainty involves Steve Schneider, described as Mr. Koresh's right-hand man. Mr. Ricks said if anyone had influence over the cult members other than Mr. Koresh, it would be Mr. Schneider. He said Mr. Schneider now spoke with officers in negotiations almost as much as Mr. Koresh.

Mr. Ricks said Mr. Koresh's testiness probably reflected something of the mood inside the compound, where members have now been holed up for a week.

"I would be most surprised if life in that compound were anywhere near normal," Mr. Ricks said.

But for law officers on the outside life here is not quite normal either as the wait drags on. One bit of gallows humor has it that Waco is actually an acronym.

Its meaning? "We Ain't Coming Out."

Warning of Violence Was Unheeded After Cult Leader's Gun Battle in '87

BY ADAM NOSSITER | MARCH 10, 1993

WACO, TEX., MARCH 9 — In a commando-style raid five and a half years ago, David Koresh and members of his insular religious sect gave the outside world a warning about his passionate attachment to firearms and his potential for violence. The outside world chose to look the other way.

The raid could have been a scene from the movie "Platoon," one of Mr. Koresh's favorites. On the morning of Nov. 3, 1987, he and seven of his followers, dressed in camouflage uniforms and combat boots, with charcoal smeared under their eyes and armed with military-style rifles and shotguns, crawled onto the sect's property east of here. Their objective seemed to be to retake the land that Mr. Koresh had left three years earlier in a dispute with the sect's leader, although Mr. Koresh and the others said they were trying to uncover evidence of illegal activity by the leader.

There was an exchange of gunfire that lasted for several minutes and left the leader, George Roden, slightly wounded, and Mr. Koresh ultimately in control of the property and the sect. But after a two-week trial here, none of the participants were convicted of anything and their weapons were returned to them.

The raid was part of a series of events that involved a disinterred corpse, efforts to resurrect the dead and the display in the courthouse here of a coffin with a skeleton inside.

But despite the peculiarities of the case and the number and type of weapons involved, the return of the guns caused no particular stir here, in a state where the ownership of more than one firearm does not necessarily raise eyebrows.

"They had a constitutional right to their guns," Dan Weyenberg, then and now McLennan County's chief deputy sheriff, said in a recent interview. "Our district attorney did not go for a seizure."

NO CONVICTION, NO SEIZURE

Under Texas law the district attorney had no such option, said John W. Segrest, now the McLennan County district attorney. "The Government can keep weapons used in a felony," he said, but without convictions, "there was really not any other choice" but to return the guns and ammunition.

Still, the firepower that Mr. Koresh and his loyalists carried on their raid was extreme even by Texas standards and inspired extreme comments.

"A McLennan County sheriff's deputy out there said at the time they had enough weapons and ammunition to hold off the entire McLennan County Sheriff's Department, the police department and the local national guard," El-Hadi J. Shabazz, an assistant district attorney who prosecuted the case, said in an interview last week.

The raiders, another prosecutor said, carried five .223-caliber semi-automatic assault rifles, two .22-caliber rifles and two 12-gauge shotguns with almost 400 rounds of ammunition. All these weapons were confiscated by the authorities.

As the case unfolded, the authorities also seized three more rifles, an additional 2,500 rounds of .223-caliber ammunition and several boxes of .22-caliber cartridges and shotgun shells. The .223-caliber guns are the same size as the powerful, high-velocity military assault rifle, the M-16.

"That was 1987," Mr. Shabazz said. "Imagine what they have in 1993."

HUGS FROM THE JURORS

In 1987, Mr. Shabazz said, there were few besides himself who seemed concerned about the steadily arming religious group 10 miles outside Waco. Morever, he said, Mr. Koresh, or Vernon Howell, as he was known then, was not perceived as any sort of threat.

Mr. Koresh maintained in his trial that he had been aiming at a tree, not trying to hit Mr. Roden. And after the jurors who heard that argument deadlocked on the charge of attempted murder, several hugged him.

His comrades, who said they had been shooting into the air, were found not guilty of the same charge.

Mr. Shabazz, now a lawyer in private practice here, did not explain why he did not seek to retry Mr. Koresh after the hung jury, although he did recall with some bitterness that "it was a black man trying to prosecute seven white men in a Southern town called Waco."

And the current District Attorney, Mr. Segrest, noted, "Howell at the time was not seen as any kind of menace."

With Mr. Koresh freed, he and other Branch Davidians were free to pursue their twin devotions, the Bible and firearms, which they did until Federal agents tried to storm their heavily armed compound nine days ago.

ROOTS OF THE RIVALRY

Mr. Roden recovered from wounds in his chest and hand. Two years later he killed a man in Odessa, Tex. He claimed the man had been sent by Mr. Koresh to kill him. Mr. Roden was found not guilty by reason of insanity and is now in the state mental hospital in Vernon, Tex.

The rivalry between Mr. Roden and Mr. Koresh over leadership of the Branch Davidians dated to the early 1980's and at various times involved sex, threats, guns and a skeleton with a pink bow around its neck.

A decade ago, when Mr. Koresh was in his early 20's and had recently arrived at the cult's compound, he began a sexual relationship with Mr. Roden's mother, Lois, then in her late 60's. She was the widow of Ben Roden, who had led the Branch Davidians, a splinter group of the Seventh-Day Adventist Church, for several years. After Mr. Roden's death in 1978, Lois Roden had assumed leadership, and their son, George, was assumed to be her successor.

George Roden, now 55 years old, soon perceived Mr. Koresh as a rival for leadership and was also offended by the relationship with his mother, former cult members say. A gun aficionado himself, Mr. Roden took to threatening Mr. Koresh. In a Federal lawsuit in 1985, he accused Mr. Koresh of raping his mother, brainwashing her and turning her against him.

The year before that lawsuit, Mr. Koresh had left the Waco compound, which the cult members call Mount Carmel, with virtually all of Mr. Roden's followers. The group went to the East Texas town of Palestine, where without a base or resources, they lived for a time like hobos in wooden shacks.

Mr. Roden seethed over Mr. Koresh's influence on the several dozen members of the sect who had followed him. And in 1987, he challenged Mr. Koresh to a ghoulish contest: whoever could bring back the dead deserved to be the true leader.

KORESH DECLINES THE CHALLENGE

People involved in the case say Mr. Roden dug up a coffin from the cemetery on the sect's grounds. Inside was the skeleton of a woman, identified in news reports at the time as that of Ana Hughes, who had died 20 years earlier. Mr. Roden put the coffin in the cult's chapel and three times tried to resurrect the woman with prayers.

Mr. Koresh did not take up the challenge. Instead, he searched for laws that Mr. Roden might be breaking. Finally, he reported to the McLennan County sheriff's office that Mr. Roden was engaging in corpse abuse.

The authorities told him to get evidence, like a photograph.

So Mr. Koresh staged his raid. Oddly, he and his seven companions neglected to take a camera along, one prosecutor said, but they did take the guns, and camouflage gear used for deer hunting, which had been purchased at the local Kmart.

They had prepared a map of the property that pinpointed where each member of the party would take up his position. They sneaked onto the grounds before dawn but waited until midafternoon before going into action.

When they found the portly, bearded Mr. Roden hiding behind a tree and armed with an Uzi semi-automatic, the battle broke out.

ODDITIES OF THE TRIAL

The trial five months later, in April 1988, is still remembered in the domed, turn-of-the-century McLennan County Courthouse for its circus atmosphere, including one particularly bizarre feature.

Mr. Koresh's lawyer wanted to introduce the coffin, complete with the skeleton, as evidence. Before the coffin was taken to the courthouse, Mr. Koresh tied a pink bow around the skeleton's neck, to dress it up.

The coffin remained closed, but it sat in the rotunda for most of the trial while the lawyers fought over whether it could be admitted as evidence. Ultimately it was not and was returned to Mount Carmel and buried.

There were other oddities. Mr. Roden, the victim and complaining witness in the trial, had to be fetched from the county jail, where he was serving a six-month sentence for contempt, because of his abusive language to a Federal judge in one of his civil suits.

The courthouse was filled with supporters of Mr. Koresh and his co-defendants. During breaks, wives would hug husbands and children would scamper about.

Denise Wilkerson, who was helping Mr. Shabazz prosecute the case, said this all had a winning effect on the jury.

And Gary Coker, who was Mr. Koresh's lawyer, recalling the effective defense he was able to mount, commented: "It was a pretty good story, pretty good. Roden was just such a bad actor. He was bad news."

After the jurors deadlocked on Mr. Koresh and found the others not guilty, Mr. Koresh invited them and the prosecutors out to Mount Carmel for ice cream. The prosecutors declined, and none of the jurors who can be found today would say whether they had attended or anything else about the case.

But if the jurors and Mr. Koresh's followers were satisfied with the outcome, Mr. Shabazz was not. To the prosecutor, the affair had looked like "a dangerous paramilitary operation" in which the participants "took the law in their own hands."

"I told the jury, 'Today it's George Roden, and who is it going to be tomorrow?' "

Cult Leader Gives 'Letter From God'

SPECIAL TO THE NEW YORK TIMES | APRIL 11, 1993

WACO, TEX., APRIL 10 — David Koresh presented the Federal authorities with a four-page "letter from God" on Friday, citing biblical passages and threatening the forces that have surrounded his religious sect's compound near here for 43 days.

Federal Bureau of Investigation officials said the letter, written in the first person as if from God and bearing no salutation, was addressed to "Friends" and was signed "Yahweh Koresh."

"The letter is threatening and cites six biblical passages," Bob Ricks, a bureau spokesman, said today. "The gist of the letter, like the biblical passages, conveys messages of a powerful, angry God empowering his chosen people to punish and harm those who oppose him."

LETTER WON'T BE MADE PUBLIC

Mr. Ricks said the letter would not be made public.

Mr. Koresh has said since March 2 that he was awaiting a message from God telling him when he and his followers in the Branch Davidian sect should leave their 77-acre compound, where they have been trapped by the authorities since a shootout on Feb. 28.

Whether the letter represents Mr. Koresh's message is uncertain, F.B.I. officials said. "We have not had confirmation from those inside that this is a message from God," Mr. Ricks said. "We're trying to get confirmation of that fact. But if it is the message from God, then we have to know what the heck the message is."

Mr. Ricks also said today that the authorities would begin surrounding the Branch Davidian complex with spirals of barbed security wire as "the next logical step to control the compound."

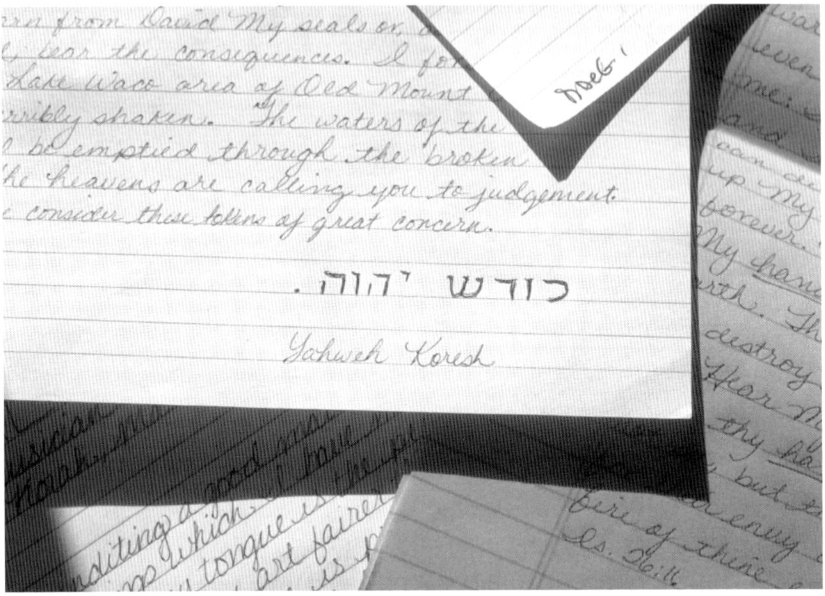

SHELLY KATZ/THE LIFE IMAGES COLLECTION/GETTY IMAGES

Details from letters dictated by Branch Davidian cult leader David Koresh as Yahweh Koresh.

NO. 2 IN SECT DELIVERS LETTER

He said those inside "seem to be more emboldened in their attempts to come out and test the control of our perimeter."

Mr. Koresh's second-in-command, Steve Schneider, was allowed out of the compound Friday to deliver the four-page "letter from God" and to ignite seven smoke flares in recognition of a Passover holy day, and there apparently was a minor incident as a result.

"Mr. Schneider, either through his own confusion or whatever, came out one occasion too many yesterday and we had to flash-bang him twice," Mr. Ricks said. "Flash-bang" is a law-enforcement term for stun grenades, which are intended to blind and disorient an opponent.

Death in Waco: A Fiery End; An Angry Telephone Call Signals the End of the World for Cult Members

BY ROSS E. MILLOY | APRIL 20, 1993

WACO, TEX., APRIL 19 — The bizarre ministry of David Koresh ended today in a hellish vision of fire and smoke every bit as nightmarish as anything he might have prophesied to his followers.

For those inside the Branch Davidian compound, the beginning of the end came with a telephone call.

At 5:55 A.M. local time, David Koresh's chief lieutenant, Steve Schneider, spoke with Federal officials and was told that if all those inside the compound did not surrender immediately, tear gas would be pumped inside.

Mr. Schneider reportedly slammed down the receiver, pulled the telephone to a doorway and hurled it out into the front yard.

THE END IS NEAR

Within minutes, armored vehicles began to smash gaping holes in the pink-and-white compound structures so that agents could pump in 15-second doses of the chemical agent CS. The end was only hours away.

For days, the Federal authorities had given more and more hints that they were tiring of the standoff. At midweek, Bob Ricks, a spokesman for the Federal Bureau of Investigation, began emphasizing at press briefings a litany of Mr. Koresh's "broken promises."

On Sunday night, agents began clearing cars, debris and scrub oak trees from areas around the compound. Though no one said so at the time, it seems clear that they were opening the way for the assault vehicles and opening up lines of sight for snipers.

Negotiations had achieved nothing since March 19, when three sect members walked out of the compound, Mr. Ricks told reporters on Saturday. He added that Mr. Koresh wanted "a showdown with the Government where massive casualties and deaths will take place."

AREA RESIDENTS WARNED

People who live near the compound had been awakened at 5 A.M. today by helicopters. Within an hour, several were visited by Department of Public Safety officers warning that an action was planned for the compound and that they should stay indoors if possible.

Just after 6 A.M., the first armored vehicle approached the southern corner of the main structure and loudspeakers began blaring a message: "This is not an assault! Do not fire! Exit the compound and follow instructions!" The vehicle was met with a volley of gunfire from within the compound.

Over the next three hours, armored vehicles slammed into the wooden frame building a dozen times, pumping in tear gas and badly damaging the exterior.

'WE WANT OUR PHONES'

At 9:10, a white sheet was unfurled from an upstairs window. In hastily scrawled orange lettering it read, "We Want Our Phones Fixed." Wispy clouds could be seen rising from the ground near the main building, possibly from some underground chamber or tunnel that had been flooded with tear gas.

Cult members continued to shoot at the advancing combat vehicles, firing several hundred rounds from various positions.

From their vantage point at a police barricade a mile and a half away, reporters could see across pastures of peacefully grazing cattle a scene of growing violence in the compound beyond. Armored vehicles crisscrossed the courtyard beneath the Branch Davidians' fluttering flag.

Just after 10 A.M., a man could be seen waving a rag from a doorway on the southeastern side of the compound. The F.B.I., believing it might be a white flag, called out to him over the loudspeaker system, "If that is a white flag, come out and surrender."

FORT WORTH STAR-TELEGRAM/TRIBUNE NEWS SERVICE/GETTY IMAGES

A ball of fire erupts from the Branch Davidian compound in Waco, Tex., as federal agents tried to drive the Davidians out of the compound.

DESTRUCTION GOES ON

There was no response from within, and the destruction of the buildings continued. Gunfire from the Branch Davidians continued sporadically but agents did not return the fire, the F.B.I. said.

Three large Chinook helicopters, ready to ferry the injured to hospitals, waited on the ground to the east of the compound, their rotors still. A small plane made slow circles in the hazy blue sky. A flock of buzzards circled just as lazily on the opposite horizon, undisturbed by the mounting chaos a few thousand yards away.

By noon, whole sections of the exterior walls had been demolished. Portions of the roof were collapsing. Cult members inside had been forced into an ever-narrowing circle of rooms. A vehicle rammed the upper story on the northeast side of the building to insert more tear gas. A few minutes later, from the same section of the building, a flicker of orange could be seen.

“Is that smoke?” a radio reporter asked the horde of journalists around him.

By 12:10 P.M., fire and smoke were pouring from one end of the building. Nearly 100 reporters and photographers, their lenses and binoculars all trained on the distant hilltop, watched in near silence as 40-mile-an-hour winds whipped the first flames into a billowing pyre.

A huge funnel of smoke swirled tornado-like above the compound, and once the fascination with the awful spectacle subsided, the journalists leaped to their cameras and telephones.

Those at the checkpoint grew increasingly uneasy as flames engulfed the compound buildings and there were no signs of an evacuation. Many people simply stood open-mouthed, staring at the seething inferno.

“My God,” murmured a reporter from Fort Worth. “It’s horrific. Horrific. A holocaust. Could anyone live through that?”

No one could answer her, yet.

Manacles of the Mind

OPINION | BY JAN JARBOE | APRIL 21, 1993

IN THE TEXAS BIBLE BELT, where I grew up and still live, religious cartoon characters such as David Koresh are the rule, not the exception. Here, all sorts of folks talk for God.

When I was a child growing up in the Southern Baptist church, the Bible was often cited as justification for the strangest behavior. Holy Scripture was the reason I couldn't go to the movies on Sunday afternoons, swim in the same pool with boys or drink from the same water fountain as black people.

Later, when I grew up and became one of the half-dozen or so liberals in the state, God's word was sometimes given as the reason I couldn't buy grapes in the grocery store, wasn't supposed to support the war machine with my taxes and was forbidden to purchase stock in predatory multinational corporations.

As I sat in my living room Monday and watched on television — live from Waco! — as 86 people, including 25 children, went up in smoke in an apocalyptic crematorium, I wondered why it often takes the fire of death to reveal religion's dark side.

David Koresh called himself a "sinful prophet," and when it came to naming his core identity, he did not lie. This was a man who gorged on sex, beer, rock 'n' roll, guns and religion. The only holiness he saw was in himself. He justified sealing himself and his followers off in a concrete compound east of Waco by personifying himself as good and the rest of the world as evil. In the end, he indulged his own internalized demons in a final orgy of violence.

David Koresh's brand of fanaticism is so common that only rarely does it make news. Many people, not just members of the Branch Davidians, feel so empty and afraid, and disillusioned with families, the economy and politics that they are willing to pay almost any price for certainty. This desire for perfection is the same the world over. It leads housewives in Greenwich, Conn., to hermetically seal off their neighborhoods and to teach their children at home rather than subject them to the dangerous ambiguity of public or even private schools.

Having just returned from a 12-day trip to Bosnia-Herzegovina, I felt the same intractable sense of savagery and doom emanating from that small country as was present in Waco before the inferno. Bosnia-Herzegovina is soaked with blood, but instead of gaining victory, all the raping, plundering and murder only fuels a morass of ethnic hatred. When I asked Muslim refugees in camps west of Sarajevo what they thought the solution to their plight was, without exception the answer was the same: “Give us guns.” There is no justice, much less peace, in fear.

Always, the road to fanaticism starts with a fine, often holy premise. For instance, a regular churchgoer becomes convinced that all life is sacred. The belief is so strong that it takes on godlike power. At this point, the person is no longer celebrating life’s sacredness but is intoxicated by the power of his own ideas. He serves his belief at all cost even when, as happened in Florida last month, it provokes the murder of a physician who performed abortions. This is the nature of fanaticism: it provokes people to do the very things they hate.

It’s easier to understand David Koresh’s behavior than it is to understand the F.B.I.’s strategy. Mr. Koresh was simply fulfilling his own prophecy. In his mind, he was good, the Government was beastly and evil and because of the unbridgeable gap between good and evil there was no way out other than death. The mistake the F.B.I. made was in battling the external compound that Mr. Koresh had erected rather than confronting the real enemy, which was his internal prison — what the poet William Blake called “the mind-forg’d manacles.”

Federal agents played the role Mr. Koresh created for them, treating him like a terrorist and his followers like hostages, not fanatics. By talking only to Mr. Koresh and his chief lieutenants, the F.B.I. agents solidified his power over his followers and made themselves and their law enforcement colleagues appear as beastly as he claimed.

The families of those who died inside the compound have a right to wonder why none of them were allowed to appeal to their relatives directly before the F.B.I. rammed the compound with tanks. If agents were creative enough to resort to blasting the compound with Tibetan chants, why didn't they try something as simple as the severed bonds of family love? Perhaps it wouldn't have changed the outcome, but at least the families would have the comfort of knowing they tried.

The public, too, was somehow complicit in forcing an end to what was constantly described in the media as the "cult standoff." There were only two other possibilities to what happened in Waco. One was for David Koresh to give up his vision of salvation — the idea that he alone could save the world — and the other was for the F.B.I. to give up the goal of getting him to surrender at all cost. Naturally, neither side was able to give in.

The tension, stretched out over 51 days, became unbearable. You could feel everyone wanting something to happen, even if it was an eruption of chaos. Among the comments I heard on Monday after the fire were these: "That'll show 'em," "Thank God it's over" and, "At least we won't be spending $1 million a day in Waco anymore." The desire for resolution was so strong that when it was relieved in fiery death, the feeling was almost thrilling.

The one person who thrived on the tension was David Koresh himself. The anxiety of others gave him the power to create his own personal apocalypse. Instead of dealing with the anger, lust, greed and hatred of his own dark side, he projected it onto the outside world and made us all part of his own private beast.

In the end, he did what spiritually diseased people always do. He refused to take responsibility for his own internal life and tried instead to dominate people and events outside himself. A true messiah dies to save others. David Koresh was no messiah. More than 90 people died to spare him the trouble of wrestling the beast that was always within himself.

JAN JARBOE is a journalist and non-fiction writer.

Koresh, on Tape, Screams About Children

BY DAVID JOHNSTON | JUNE 10, 1993

WASHINGTON, JUNE 9 — As a furious gun battle raged at the Branch Davidian cult's compound in Texas, the group's leader, David Koresh, telephoned the Waco police, screaming, "You killed some of my children."

"There is a bunch of us dead and a bunch of you guys dead now — that's your fault," Mr. Koresh yelled as Federal agents from the Bureau of Alcohol, Tobacco and Firearms stormed the Branch Davidian compound outside Waco.

Mr. Koresh's words were recorded after he called the police emergency number and talked with Larry Lynch, a lieutenant in the sheriff's office who can be heard calmly trying to persuade him to stop shooting at the agents and provide a count of the number of wounded cult members.

The 30-minute tape, part of 30 hours of tape recordings made at the time of the raid, was played publicly for the first time today at a hearing of a House Appropriations subcommittee investigating the performance of Federal agents in the raid.

TALKING FROM THE START

The abortive raid on Feb. 28 left four Federal agents dead and 16 wounded. Several cult members were also killed and wounded. The shootout led to the 51-day siege culminating in the tear gas assault by the Federal Bureau of Investigation that resulted in a disastrous fire. More than 70 cult members died, including at least 17 children.

"Who am I speaking with?" asked Mr. Lynch during the exchange.

"The notorious," answered Mr. Koresh. "What did you guys do that for?"

Mr. Lynch replied: "What I'm doing is I'm trying to establish some communications links with you."

"No, no, no, no, no, let me tell you something." Mr. Koresh said. "You see, you brought a bunch of guys out here and you killed some of my children. We told you we wanted to talk."

As Mr. Lynch tried to persuade Mr. Koresh to stop shooting and provide a count of his followers who were wounded, Mr. Koresh responded with a tangled but eerily calm theological lecture. "See, we will serve God first," he said. "Now we will serve the God of the church. Now we are willing and we've been willing all this time to sit down with anybody."

The tape provided ambiguous hints of Mr. Koresh's foreknowledge of the raid — a factor that officials have cited as the main reason the assault went disastrously awry.

Ronald K. Noble, an official of the Treasury Department, of which the firearms bureau is a unit, testified at the hearing that Federal agents went ahead even though they were under explicit orders to abort the raid if they had any reason to believe they had lost the element of surprise.

Other agency officials testified that they were satisfied that Mr. Koresh was unaware of their operation when they authorized the raid. One official said the agents expected all the cult members' weapons to be stored inside a single room, but instead encountered what he estimated were 40 armed cult members in firing positions.

CLAIMS AND DOUBTS

Representative Steny H. Hoyer, a Maryland Democrat who is chairman of the panel, said he did not believe Mr. Koresh's vague statements on the tape, which hint that the cult leader knew both that Federal authorities had an undercover agent inside the compound and that he had advance knowledge of the raid.

"We knew you were coming and everything," said Mr. Koresh. "You see we knew before you even knew."

Once Mr. Lynch sought to interrupt Mr. Koresh's religious preaching to negotiate a cease-fire so the Federal agents could rescue one of their wounded.

"We can talk theology but not right now," said Mr. Lynch.

Mr. Koresh replied: "No, this is life. This is life and death."

Mr. Lynch responded, "That's what I'm talking about."

Mr. Koresh answered, "Theology is life and death."

CHAPTER 4

Marshall Applewhite: Heaven's Gate

The 39 members of Heaven's Gate believed they were taking a celestial journey to a better world. But in the end, they took only their own lives in the largest mass suicide in the United States. The 1997 exodus was organized by Marshall Applewhite, the group's leader. A former music teacher, Applewhite's ideas changed over the nearly 25 years he proselytized. But one idea persisted: Those who followed his doctrine would ascend to spaceships, enter new bodies — those of extraterrestrials — and enjoy a new life. He and his small but fervent flock of long-time followers recorded farewell statements and made what Applewhite called their "final exit."

Leader Believed in Space Aliens and Apocalypse

BY FRANK BRUNI | MARCH 28, 1997

BEFORE HE BEGAN his ultimately suicidal mission as an extraterrestrial shepherd to lead the chosen aboard a spaceship into eternity, Marshall Herff Applewhite lived an apparently unremarkable life in Houston as a music professor who nurtured the choir at his Episcopal church.

That was in the early 1970's, and people who knew him then said they saw no omens of the zealot Mr. Applewhite would become. But for reasons that were unclear, and with a suddenness that was equally mystifying, he was seemingly transformed into someone else from 1972

BROOKS KRAFT/SYGMA/GETTY IMAGES

Marshall Herff Applewhite, founder of the religious group Heaven's Gate, speaking on videotape.

to 1975, a budding cult leader with beliefs in aliens and Armageddon.

Mr. Applewhite and a female companion, refashioning themselves first as Bo and Peep, and later as Do and Ti, set off on a nomadic adventure through the Midwest and West, preaching their unorthodox gospel and beckoning people to prepare with them for an ascent into the stars. It was that journey that apparently led to what happened inside a million-dollar house in Rancho Santa Fe, Calif., where the bodies of 39 cult members, who had committed suicide, were found on Wednesday.

Late yesterday, the authorities determined that the body of Mr. Applewhite, 65 years old, was among those recovered from the house. There seems to be little question that the people in the house were disciples of Mr. Applewhite's preachings, which were accessible on the Internet and were being actively spread in public lectures by his followers as recently as last year, according to one writer who has done extensive research on Mr. Applewhite and his cult.

"He went underground for a long time, but then in the last two years, posters for his group began appearing in cities where New Age stuff was prominent," said the writer, Peter Klebnikov, who is researching a book on doomsday cults.

Mr. Klebnikov said the posters, which summoned people to special lectures, articulated a spiritual philosophy and apocalyptic outcome identical to those espoused through the years by Mr. Applewhite, and warned that the end was near.

According to various newspaper and magazine articles about Mr. Applewhite, his father was a Presbyterian minister, and Mr. Applewhite studied to become a minister but then switched his focus to music.

He received a master's degree in music from the University of Colorado at Boulder in 1969, published reports said. While there, he played starring roles in two musicals, "Oklahoma!" and "South Pacific."

At some point, he married and had two children, Mr. Klebnikov said. Mr. Applewhite also went to Alabama and taught music at the University of Alabama, published reports said.

By 1971, he had apparently divorced, left his family and moved to Texas, which may have been where he was born. Tom Crow, an organist at St. Mark's Episcopal Church in Houston, where Mr. Applewhite worked from 1971 to 1972, said yesterday that he believed Mr. Applewhite had been raised near Corpus Christi.

In Houston, Mr. Applewhite worked for several years as a music professor at St. Thomas University and sang 15 roles with the Houston Grand Opera, said a New York Times Magazine profile of him and his group in February 1976. He also directed the choir at St. Mark's.

"He was a superb musician, a superb singer and a super choir director," Mr. Crow said, adding that Mr. Applewhite was an "extraordinarily gentle fellow" whose patience seemed ideal for teaching.

Mr. Crow said that Mr. Applewhite had occasionally displayed a curiosity in meditation and Eastern mysticism but that it was nothing out of the ordinary.

"I wouldn't have seen any preview of any of the cult business that finally happened," Mr. Crow said.

Its genesis seems to have come in 1972, when Mr. Applewhite, then about 40, met a nurse named Bonnie Lu Nettles, then 44, and the two discovered a mutual interest in astrology and reincarnation and came to believe that they were the earthly incarnations of aliens.

Materials put on the Internet by the Heaven's Gate cult group, which the authorities have named in connection with the mass suicide, give this version of the meeting of Mr. Applewhite and Ms. Nettles:

"In the early 1970's, two members of the Kingdom of Heaven (or what some might call two aliens from space) incarnated into two unsuspecting humans in Houston. The registered nurse was happily married with four children, worked in the nursery of a local hospital, and enjoyed a small astrology practice. The music professor, who had lived with a male friend for some years, was contentedly involved in cultural and academic activities."

The Internet text continues, "They consciously recognized that they were sent from space to do a task that had something to do with the Bible."

The couple opened a short-lived book store in Houston called the Christian Arts Center, which sold information on astrology, metaphysics and Theosophy.

Then, according to the group's own writings, published reports and experts familiar with the cult started by Mr. Applewhite and Ms. Nettles, they began to take retreats during which they formulated their beliefs.

Mr. Klebnikov said they had set up a spiritual retreat of sorts in a house in Houston that they called Knowplace. Calling themselves Bo and Peep, they also traveled outside Texas to share their philosophy with others.

In August 1974, they were arrested in Harlingen, Tex., on charges of stealing credit cards and a car, according to the magazine profile of Mr. Applewhite.

Both that article and the cult's own Internet materials said the credit cards belonged to the husband of a woman who had left home to join Bo and Peep.

The Internet materials said Mr. Applewhite was extradited to St. Louis, from which the car had been taken, but the authorities there could not provide details about the disposition of the case yesterday.

It did not put an end to either Mr. Applewhite's travels or his proselytizing. In 1975, he and Ms. Nettles were preaching in Oregon, and they attracted national attention after persuading a group of about 20 people from the tiny coastal town of Waldport to sever all ties to the lives they were leading and make a pilgrimage to the prairie of eastern Colorado, where they would supposedly rendezvous with a space ship.

The notoriety that the incident brought them, and growing scrutiny by Federal authorities and cult watchers, scared them underground for a long time after that, said Mr. Klebnikov. Mr. Crow, the organist in Houston, said that while people in Houston heard from Mr. Applewhite occasionally until 1975, they lost track of him at that point.

The group's Internet materials, which refer to Mr. Applewhite and Ms. Nettles as Do and Ti and as "The Two," said they and their followers went into deliberate seclusion for 17 years, until 1992. Ms. Nettles apparently died of cancer in 1985.

In those years of relative silence, Mr. Klebnikov said, they moved many times, usually throughout the West. Sometimes they lived in motels, sometimes in rented houses, sometimes in wilderness camps.

Jerome Clark, author of "The U.F.O. Encyclopedia," said that wherever they were, Bo and Peep kept careful track of their sheep, monitoring their followers' movements and their adherence to an ascetic life style, dressing them in odd uniforms and giving them "psychic training."

"Sometimes they were told to sit and stare at a single object for hours," Mr. Clark said.

The group showed up in places as disparate as Salt Lake City, Santa Fe, N.M., and Laramie, Wyo. Dr. Leo Sprinkle, an emeritus professor of counseling service at the University of Wyoming and a researcher of U.F.O. experiences, recalled meeting Bo and Peep in Laramie when they spoke to his group, the Institute for U.F.O. Contactees Studies.

"They thought those of us that were doing U.F.O research did not have the full story that they had," Dr. Sprinkle said. "They were attempting to attract people who would go with them."

To survive, the members of the group did odd jobs or used the money that rich recruits brought with them. Mr. Clark said that the group bought houses in the Denver area and the Dallas area and called these houses "crafts," as in space crafts.

In 1993, according to the group's Internet materials, "we took a much more overt step toward the conclusion of our task." The group said it published an advertisement in USA Today that year that was titled "U.F.O. Cult Resurfaces with Final Offer," along with advertisements in other publications that proclaimed, "Last Chance to Advance Beyond Human."

"Again, the ball was rolling," the group said. "We were definitely in the public eye."

In 1994 and 1995, newspaper reports from various cities cite controversial public lectures by the group, then identifying itself as Total Overcomers, in which its followers talked about the coming end of the world and the need for people to renounce worldly belongings and desires.

But what is unclear from those reports, and what cult experts seemed uncertain about, was whether Mr. Applewhite made any of these appearances or emerged in public himself. The question of whether he was still tending to his flock, however, was resolved by the presence of his body among the dozens of other corpses in Rancho Santa Fe.

Families Learning of 39 Cultists Who Died Willingly

BY B. DRUMMOND AYRES JR. | MARCH 29, 1997

AFTER FIELDING MORE than 1,500 telephone calls from anguished relatives across the country in the last 24 hours, investigators said today that they had identified 30 of the 39 members of a millennialist cult who had committed mass suicide in a hillside house here.

Officials of the San Diego County Sheriff's Office released the names to the public this evening and pleaded for help in identifying the remaining 9 bodies.

At the same time, investigators disclosed that about a half-dozen of the 18 men of the cult who died had been surgically castrated, including Marshall Herff Applewhite, 65 and the group's leader. The group demanded celibacy of its members and avoided any suggestion of sensuality.

At an afternoon news conference, Brian Blackbourne, the Chief Medical Examiner, said the castrations appeared to have been done some time well in the past and had been carried out with satisfactory surgical skill. He offered no other details or explanations of the finding.

The bodies of the group, identified by the authorities as Heaven's Gate, were discovered in the house on Wednesday, scattered on their backs on cots and mattresses. All but two had purple cloths over their heads and shoulders like shrouds. Most of them had died of suffocation. Plastic bags had apparently been placed over their heads after they had ingested a potent mix of phenobarbital and alcohol.

According to material the group posted on its Internet site, the timing of the suicides were probably related to the arrival of the Hale-Bopp comet, which members seemed to regard as a cosmic emissary beckoning them to another world.

As the authorities went about the task of notifying and talking with relatives of the victims today, a farewell videotape made by the cult members suggested that they had gone to their deaths quite willingly, some even joyfully.

"We couldn't be happier about what we're going to do," one woman said, her voice choking a bit but her face anything but sad. Another woman, smiling, added, "We are all happy to be doing what we are doing."

A toll-free number set up by the police prompted many relatives to call, already suspecting the worst because, in many cases, their loved ones had been away or out of contact for months or even years. Other relatives called after excerpts of the tape, in which pairs of cult members spoke, one after another, were broadcast over national television.

"Most of the families are breaking down when we talk to them," said Calvin Vine, an investigator from the San Diego County Medical Examiner's Office. By contrast, there was a tear or two on the farewell tape, but they seemed almost tears of joy.

The authorities said that although they were dealing with a mass suicide almost without parallel in the United States, it appeared to be nothing more than that, with no suspicious criminal elements.

"We are proceeding with the preliminary conclusion that what we are looking at is, in fact, 39 suicides," said one investigator, Jack Drown, a San Diego County undersheriff.

Yet Mr. Drown conceded that it might never be known just what kind of mindset had led the members of the group to shut themselves up in the house and then consume lethal combinations of vodka and phenobarbitol.

"I'm not too sure we will ever have satisfactory answers," he said.

The group had lived quietly, almost unnoticed in this upscale community, with members spending much of their time designing computer programs for various commercial clients.

Mark Applewhite, the son of the group's leader, said in a letter addressed to "anyone hurt by the actions of Marshall Herff Applewhite" and given to KZTV, a CBS affiliate in Corpus Christi, Tex., that he was "deeply hurt by the knowledge that people have now lost their lives in connection with my father." Saying he had not seen his father since he

DAVID MCNEW/GETTY IMAGES

The 39 members of the religious group Heaven's Gate willingly committed suicide in their Rancho Santa Fe, Calif., mansion, on March 27, 1997. Each was covered with a purple shroud and wore Nike sneakers.

was 5, the son said he was a born-again Christian and hoped that God would take the "terrible news" and turn it into a message of hope.

Investigators also disclosed today that the cult, which had a nomadic history in this country, might have been planning a trip abroad. They said that while checking the house, they had found a map plastered to a wall with markings that indicated the course of an overseas journey. The investigators did not elaborate.

The farewell tape, broadcast by ABC television, was especially striking for its upbeat tone, considering what lay ahead for those speaking and peering into the camera. On it, one cult member — none identified themselves — said his death would bring him "just the happiest day of my life," and added, "I've been looking forward for this for so long."

A woman who appeared to be in her 20's looked intently into the camera and said, grinning broadly, "We are all choosing of our own free will to go to the next level."

Another woman said, "We just wish you could all be here and doing what we are doing."

The tone of that farewell tape, made with the cult members sitting in pairs on chairs placed outside in a setting of trees and bushes, was similar to the tone of another tape found after the 39 bodies were discovered, with men and women alike dressed all in black, their hair closely cropped and their faces covered by diamond-shaped purple cloths.

On the second tape, Marshall Applewhite tried to explain why he and the others were about to take their lives. He said that human bodies were just temporary earthly parking places for the soul and that suicide would free the soul to make a rendezvous on a higher plane of existence with an unidentified flying object that is trailing the Hale-Bopp comet, now on a swing past Earth.

"We have no hesitation to leave this place, to leave the bodies that we have," Mr. Applewhite concluded.

Late today, the coroners had completed 21 of the autopsies, and medical examiners said they were prepared to release some bodies to relatives as early as this weekend. Relatives were told that they did not need to come to San Diego to claim their loved ones but could instead have mortuaries arrange shipments.

While the cult members may have taken many of their secrets to the grave, the authorities said today that they were confident that the people who died here were the only active members of the group.

"We have been told that this is not a splinter group," said Jerry Lipscomb, a San Diego County homicide detective. "We see no other tie. They are not a splinter group. They are not a group that controls any other."

The authorities provided further details of the elaborate planning that went into the suicides.

Dr. Blackbourne described one document, found by detectives, that was titled "The Routine." It outlined how the cult members were to go about killing themselves.

First, it said, 15 of the 39 cult members, called "classmates," would kill themselves with help from 8 "assistants." Then 15 more "classmates" and 8 more "assistants" would repeat the process.

It was unclear how the final 9 cult members were to go about killing themselves. To bring on death, the cult members were to ingest a dose of Dramamine, followed by "tea & toast," followed an hour later by "alco. & med."

When the bodies of the cult members were searched, Dr. Blackbourne said, the pockets of their matching black tunics were found to contain a collection of odd items — $5 bills, rolls of quarters, tubes of lip balm, pencils and ballpoint pens, and facial tissue. Beside each body was a travel bag. But Dr. Blackbourne said he had not been told what the bags contained.

These New York Times reporters and photographers contributed to the coverage of the Heaven's Gate cult: **GUSTAV NIEBUHR**, **TODD S. PURDUM**, **TIM GOLDEN**, **CAREY GOLDBERG**, **B. DRUMMOND AYRES JR.**, **JAMES STERNGOLD**, **JAMES BROOKE**, **BARRY BEARAK**, **BERNARD WEINRAUB**, **ALLEN R. MYERSON**, **KEITH BRADSHER**, **DAVID M. HERSZENHORN**, **DON TERRY**, **VIVIAN S. TOY**, **JACQUES STEINBERG**, **JOHN T. MCQUISTON**, **FRANK BRUNI**, **JIM WILSON** and **MICHAEL SHAVEL**.

Also contributing were **VERNE G. KOPYTOFF**, **CHRISTINE BIEDERMAN**, **DEAN NELSON**, **DAN DORFMAN**, **LAURAINE MILLER**, **SHELLY REESE**, **JESSE MCKINLEY**, **MICHAEL SORKIN** and **ROD PAUL**.

Gateway to Madness

EDITORIAL | BY THE NEW YORK TIMES | MARCH 29, 1997

THE EARNEST FIGURES speaking to us from the videotape are haunting in their gentleness, their sincerity, their hapless desire to have us understand that they were not crazy people, not in the clutches of some messianic madman, not the least bit nervous about their freely made decision to commit collective suicide, or, as they would put it, leave the physical "containers" they had been wearing and ascend to the Level Above Human. Only the occasional glassy expression, the naive preachiness, the supportive tittering by some of the cultists hinted at the underlying pathology that led such seemingly bright and articulate people to a tragic misjudgment.

Some find it shocking that a technically gifted group, earning its keep by designing web sites for businesses, could fall prey to aberrational beliefs that blended far-out science fiction with elements of Christianity. Members concluded that the Comet Hale-Bopp was a "marker" signaling that their time had come, a celestial omen that may even have been hiding a giant spaceship behind it, poised to carry believers to the higher level from which some claim to have originated.

But technical expertise is no proof against bizarre beliefs. Some of the most fervent believers in visits by alien spaceships and in versions of Creation that defy everything known to science have backgrounds in engineering or other technical subjects. Nor does a deep sense of spirituality protect cultists from suicidal acts that are condemned by most religions.

Experts on cult behavior are already exploring what might have led this particular group to its carefully planned, artfully choreographed ending. They will be examining the dynamics of an isolated group, the backgrounds of its members, the allure of its leader and the role of the Internet and web browsers in spreading and reinforcing bizarre theories. Fans of the web resist any suggestion that instantaneous communications have enabled paranoiacs and conspiracy theorists to loft and expand their theories with warp speed. But events as serious as this one and as silly as the rantings of Pierre Salinger suggest that the web may exert a multiplier effect.

There was an old-fashioned element to the psychiatric-spiritual saga of Bo and Peep, who mutated into Ti and Do and piped their wounded, foolish followers to early graves. This group, like others over the long course of human history, looked for its destiny in the heavens and found it in the rantings of a madman about a ball of dirty ice with a luminous tail, the Comet Hale-Bopp. As the world approaches a new millennium, a time when cosmic soul-searching intensifies, other groups will look skyward and some, alas, may seek salvation in acts the rest of us consider lunacy.

Cults differ from mainstream faiths in their lack of ancient roots and their glorification of hubris. Resurrection, the meaninglessness of the flesh, the primacy of the spirit, the conversion from the physical to the heavenly plane are features of several faiths. But the crucial safety brake in most theologies is that the believer himself cannot choose the moment of ascension. Only the central deity can do that.

The interesting thing about Branch Davidians, Jonestownsians and now the Heaven's Gaters is not so much their ad hoc mumbo-jumbo. It is instead the centrality of the cult figure who manages to convince the weak and wounded that he or she has acquired the godlike power to set the date and destination of life's last journey.

Letters to the Editor

THE NEW YORK TIMES | APRIL 5, 1997

ABANDONING THE SELF

To the Editor:

"Gateway to Madness" (editorial, March 29) addresses only one of the reasons for the proliferation of suicidal cults in this millenarian age. While it is true that the centrality of the cult figure who manipulates his followers is a necessary ingredient, this does not by itself explain the willingness of 39 members of the Heaven's Gate cult to end their lives. A more significant cause is a growing tendency in modern society towards the abandonment of the self in favor of a larger collectivity.

Considering that the continued survival of democracy depends on the participation of free-thinking individuals, this can only be considered alarming. Many cults loudly proclaim their support of democracy, but in truth they have little interest in protecting the individuality of their own members.

K. GORDON NEUFELD, Vancouver, Canada, March 30, 1997

CULTISTS' TRAGEDY DEFIES OUR UNDERSTANDING

To the Editor:

"Gateway to Madness" (editorial, March 29) deplores the decision by members of the Heaven's Gate cult to commit collective suicide. You observe that in most faiths "the crucial safety brake" is that "the believer himself cannot choose the moment of ascension." Proponents of physician-assisted suicide would arrogate to physicians the divine power "to set the date and destination of life's last journey." The tragedy that took place in Rancho Santa Fe, Calif., is the tragedy of suicide: whether assisted or unassisted, individual or collective.

WILLIAM J. TOOHY, New York, March 31, 1997

In Serene Setting in California, a Suicide Investigation Unfolds

BY TODD S. PURDUM | MARCH 30, 1997

FROM THE MOMENT Deputy Robert Brunk of the San Diego County Sheriff's office pulled up to the big house on the hill on Wednesday afternoon, he knew something was wrong. The drapes were pulled, the windows were closed and the outdoor lights were burning in the sunshine.

And as Deputy Brunk — responding to an anonymous 911 call about a possible group suicide — approached a side door, he sensed the unmistakable stench of death. Dreading his instincts and hoping against hope, he radioed his partner, Laura Gacek, and waited.

Together, the deputies moved through a silent hallway, a kitchen and a breakfast room, seeing nothing amiss. Then, in the central hall, they saw the first body on a cot, then 2 more, then 4 more, until they stopped at 10. They notified their commanders, put on surgical masks and gloves and went methodically through the seven-bedroom house, counting 39 bodies in all.

"It was one of the most bizarre things you'd ever expect to see," Deputy Gacek recalled on Friday with the dead-eyed aplomb of Frances McDormand in "Fargo."

"It was," Deputy Brunk said, "a very calm, serene setting — "

"Surreal," Deputy Gacek said.

Surreal only begins to sum up the story that has unfolded in the 72 hours since the deputies opened the door of 18241 Colina Norte, with 35 of the bodies publicly identified as of today. It is a tale of lost souls, of cult members estranged from their families and living a monastic, nomadic life that took some of them through a 20-year odyssey across the American West before they came to this Southern California paradise to die. Others had joined in the last year.

But for the members of the Heaven's Gate cult who swallowed

vodka and barbiturates or smothered themselves with plastic bags in meticulous stages starting as long as a week ago, death was nothing to be feared. Instead, according to the testimony they left, glowing like some ultra-modern illuminated manuscript on a home page on the Internet, it was the first step in a millennial flight to the heavenly "Level Above Human."

Their desired transport was sleek: a spaceship trailing in the wake of the Hale-Bopp comet that was so visible in the clear desert skies here when they started taking their lives. But their preparations were simple: rolls of quarters and $5 bills stuffed in the patch pockets of their black tunic-style shirts and flight-bags of belongings laid out beside them.

The group's lodgings in the sprawling Spanish-style house they rented — in a semi-rural area of eucalyptus trees and hillside scrub made lush by winter rain — contained a map of the world, studded with colored pins that detectives said appeared to mark their desired destinations on Earth, as well as pictures of alien figures suggesting their outer-worldly ambitions.

About one-third of the 18 men who died were castrated, in enforced adherence to the celibate life style the group espoused. But these monks supported their existence not by making wine or honey but by designing commercial home pages on the World Wide Web. Their clients included a local polo club and a British automobile parts dealer, and by all accounts, they did their work well.

"They were genuinely very nice people and very talented," Tom Goodspeed, the general manager of the San Diego Polo Club, told reporters this week. "But we used to joke in the beginning that they were beamed down from somewhere."

Some of those who knew them best, including former group members and the family members who had not heard from them in years, were not shocked by their final fate.

By late this morning, the parents of only one of the dead, Erika Ernst, arrived at the coroner's office in a motor home with license plates from Alberta, Canada, apparently to make arrangements to claim her body, and left an hour later. Officials have told families there was no reason to come and that local morticians can handle the task.

About 12 hours after Deputies Brunk and Gacek made their discovery, detectives from the sheriff's office were in a Beverly Hills police station, interviewing the man who made the anonymous call about the deaths.

Richard Ford, a former member of the cult initially described only by the pseudonym Rio, had left it to work for a company that makes home pages for the Internet. After receiving two videotaped messages from his former colleagues on Tuesday announcing their intentions, he drove here the next day with his new employer, then alerted the authorities, who came calling on him in the middle of the night.

"He didn't cry or anything," Lieut. Gerald L. Lipscomb, head of homicide for the San Diego Sheriff's office, recalled in an interview. "He said, 'You know, I feel badly for those people, but I'm not surprised.' "

Under the leadership of Marshall Herff Applewhite, a onetime Episcopalian choirmaster who also sang with the Houston Grand Opera, the cult had moved around the country for two decades. The reasons for arriving in this particular place remain unclear, but the authorities speculated that it might have been a prime viewing spot for the comet's brush past Earth.

What is clear is that the cult owed its tenancy in a palatial estate out of keeping with its philosophy to the financial trouble of the home's owner, Sam Koutchesfahani, an Iranian entrepreneur from a wealthy family who was in trouble with the law.

For the last 10 months, according to his lawyer, Milton J. Silverman, Mr. Koutchesfahani has been cooperating with Federal prosecutors and working as an informer in a bribery investigation of local college officials. Last year, he pleaded guilty to tax evasion and fraud charges after admitting that he took up to $350,000 from Middle Eastern students over six years, ending in 1995.

Prosecutors said he had used the money to bribe instructors at three San Diego area colleges to illegally enroll students and certify them as California residents.

Mr. Silverman said that Mr. Koutchesfahani owed $150,000 in penalties arising from the case and that he expected to sell the house to help pay them. He was eager enough to sell that his real estate agent's glossy brochure said "seller will entertain offers between $1.2 million and $1.6 million," yet the house drew no buyers — despite its tennis court, swimming pool, putting green, rose garden, elevator and citrus grove.

"An agent contacted Sam and said, 'We know someone you can rent the property to,' " Mr. Silverman recalled, adding that the group had rented a large house nearby and produced good references.

"It was true, for example, living arrangements were unusual," Mr. Silverman conceded. "There was between 20 and 40 people there. But you go back and read the Book of Acts and you look at the early Christian church, or you look at some of the other types of fundamentalist movements — and I don't mean recent, I mean the Shakers — those were their religious beliefs."

He added, "People seemed genuine, sincere — they seemed loving."

Last October, the group installed itself in the house, filling it with folding tables, computer equipment, metal bunk beds and cheap plastic lawn chairs arranged in a semi-circle in one large room that appeared to have been used for meetings.

Stella Nixon, the house's former owner who sold it to Mr. Koutchesfahani several years ago, said she was appalled to see a coroner's videotape of the victims lying under purple shrouds, their Spartan attire and catch-as-catch-can furniture contrasting with the elaborate rose-colored swags and window treatments she had chosen for the bedrooms.

Mr. Silverman said the group paid its $7,000 monthly rent in cash and eschewed Social Security numbers and banks. But the County Medical Examiner's office had a list with Social Security numbers for almost all of the group's members, and Cory VanKleeck, the manager of the Postal Annex mail service where the group maintained a box, said members called four times on March 20, frantic to know whether a bank statement had arrived.

Lieutenant Lipscomb said detectives had not yet reviewed any bank or telephone records, or information on the computers in the house, which are to be analyzed next week with the F.B.I.

For all the attention that has descended on this quiet hamlet since midweek, and for all the work of detectives and medical examiners, some answers have come slowly. Indeed, the authorities here make it plain, whatever their personal fascination, their professional curiosity is limited, because no crime appears to have been committed.

"Our purpose is to close this case, and not get involved in any cult investigation," said Lieutenant Lipscomb of the sheriff's office.

"From the beginning, we approached this investigation as if it were a homicide, in terms of securing the evidence," he said. That concern, he added, as well as concerns about who owned the house, caused a delay of several hours after the deputies' cursory look while detectives obtained a search warrant.

As it turns out, Lieutenant Lipscomb said, "There's nothing in this investigation that would suggest anything but" mass suicide.

Identification of the bodies was easy, because each had a passport, driver's license, birth certificate or other documents nearby, and the county authorities who set up a special telephone line for families with missing members were flooded by more than 100 calls a half-hour at the start. The authorities have withheld the names of only the four whose families have not been notified.

The task of determining the cause of death fell to Dr. Blackbourne, a cheery, bearded man who was formerly the chief medical examiner of Massachusetts and the deputy chief for the District of Columbia, who helped handle the bodies from the crash of an Air Florida jet into the snowy Potomac River in 1982.

But this, too, was comparatively easy, because the members left scraps of recipes and instructions, including some in a spiral notebook that read: "Proc. # 1. (maybe dramamine) tea & toast, 1 hr. before alco. & med. (10 or 12) choc. Pudding (4 oz. And powder) more alcohol."

Autopsies have shown that all of the victims died after ingesting lethal doses or phenobarbital mixed with vodka, or of asphyxiation, with plastic bags around their heads or of a combination. A 72-year-old woman from Colorado, Jacqueline Opal Leonard, had severely swollen ankles, an apparent sign of congestive heart failure, Dr. Blackbourne said. A wheelchair stood near her bed.

Yet for all the mystery surrounding the members other-worldly motivation, officials said the facts of the deaths could hardly be simpler. Still, there was nothing at all ordinary about this week in Rancho Santa Fe, as Deputy Gacek made plain.

"We see so many different things in our line of work," she said, but added, "You never think you're going to show up for work and encounter something as major as this."

These New York Times reporters and photographers contributed to the coverage of the Heaven's Gate cult: **B. DRUMMOND AYRES JR.**, **BARRY BEARAK**, **PAM BELLUCK**, **KEITH BRADSHER**, **JAMES BROOKE**, **FRANK BRUNI**, **CAREY GOLDBERG**, **TIM GOLDEN**, **ABBY GOODNOUGH**, **DAVID M. HERSZENHORN**, **JOHN T. MCQUISTON**, **ALLEN R. MYERSON**, **GUSTAV NIEBUHR**, **MIRTA OJITO**, **TODD S. PURDUM**, **KIT R. ROANE**, **JONATHAN RABINOVITZ**, **MICHAEL SHAVEL**, **JACQUES STEINBERG**, **JAMES STERNGOLD**, **DON TERRY**, **VIVIAN S. TOY**, **BERNARD WEINRAUB** and **JIM WILSON**.

Also contributing were **DEBRA BEACHY**, **CHRISTINE BIEDERMAN**, **DAN DORFMAN**, **VERNE G. KOPYTOFF**, **JESSE MCKINLEY**, **LAURAINE MILLER**, **DEAN NELSON**, **ROD PAUL**, **SHELLY REESE**, **MINDY SINK** and **MICHAEL SORKIN**.

Heaven's Gate Fit in With New Mexico's Offbeat Style

BY CAREY GOLDBERG | MARCH 31, 1997

TWO MILES UP a rutted red dirt road here lies a quixotic little kingdom of rubber tires.

It was this Spartan 40-acre camp in a silent ponderosa forest, neighbors and the authorities believe, that served as the final New Mexico staging platform for members of the Heaven's Gate cult before they set out for the California luxury estate where they chose to die.

Reflecting months of painstaking work in 1995, the compound here includes walls of piled tires, jumbles of loose tires, a large metal warehouse-like building and a roofless, five-room house built of tires packed with dirt and stacked tightly together in an architectural style not unusual in the area, known as an "Earth Ship." Many of the tires are chalk-marked "EB," which the compound's current owner believes was a designation of praise for the most diligent cult members: Early bird.

Early birds they were, said acquaintances of the cult members here. Like so many others, those acquaintances are baffled by the beliefs that drove these apparently pleasant, hard-working people to commit meticulously planned suicides.

"I hope they caught their spaceship," Larry Gustin, owner of Gustin's Hardware store in nearby Mountainair, said sympathetically. In 1995, Mr. Gustin rented three offices adjacent to his store to the group for their computer work; at the same time, they built and lived in their compound.

Others recalled some odd encounters with the group. Eddie Castillo, owner of the EJJM Gold Nugget grocery store, just north of Manzano, said that one female member had asked him to guide her through the Manzano Mountains to a crater she said was the site of a spaceship landing. He declined.

And Mike Dew, the bushy-bearded preacher of Prophetic Voices in the Wilderness, a local fundamentalist church, said today that he had once entered into a 45-minute scriptural duel with a group member known as Brother Logan Lahson — whose real name was John M. Craig — and become convinced that demonic forces were influencing the group.

Mr. Craig "would look over his shoulder as if he were consulting with a physical entity and then he would speak to me as if he were taking the words from this being," Mr. Dew said. "It was a pervading form of darkness, not a red devil with horns."

But in New Mexico's peaks and deserts, including these scrubby hills and high plains 60 miles southeast of Albuquerque, where there are so many alternative groups, the cult members struck residents as essentially normal.

In the immediate area of Manzano and Mountainair alone, residents said, there has been a Hindu retreat; a center for Russian mysticism; at least one survivalist enclave; the Sufi Foundation, a nearby retreat for those who practice Islamic mysticism, and New Age encampments for what some locals call "burned-out people."

One paramilitary group here has sought to secede from the country, residents said. And among the well-known figures in Mountainair (population 1,200) is Larry Crow, who pleaded guilty last year to knowing about a plot to blow up Oklahoma abortion clinics and welfare offices in 1995.

"To tell the truth," one longtime Mountainair resident said, "we've got nuttier people in town than those people were."

"The state has been full of those different people for years," said Carlos Sanchez, a retired accountant who has a weekend cabin at the base of the dirt road up to the compound. "They come and they love it in the mountains. No one bothers them. The local people keep very to themselves."

As did the cult members. The current owner of the compound site, Jim Thorsen, has told The Albuquerque Tribune that he believes the cult had planned to build an elaborate commune. He said the group had sold him the 40-acre site in April 1996 without giving a reason, just 10 months after they had bought it. He also said they had told him that they had planned to construct a bakery, pharmacy, lookout tower, "nutrilab" and "consuming area" and that they had planned to live in the "Earth Ship" structure made of tires and masonry.

The compound also includes a mess hall, kitchen, showers and bathrooms. Once a summer camp for an insurance company, it also has a baseball diamond and basketball court.

Though the tire construction may look like sinister barricades, it is a form of architecture that has caught on somewhat here in the Southwest; tires are recycled to provide the base for thick walls that are later plastered over. The Heaven's Gate group left behind a how-to book on the style called "Earth Ship: How to Build Your Own" (Solar Survival Press).

Leroy Herrera, a neighbor, watched group members haul their construction materials in a big old yellow truck all summer in 1995, he said, and though they once asked to rent his cement mixer, they seemed to do everything on their own.

But they did ask for help when they needed more phone lines for their computer business. Mr. Gustin said the members of the cult who rented offices from him from July to October in 1995 — under the name "Computer Knowmad" — said they had had to "come down from the mountains" to have six lines added to their three existing lines, he said, and proved themselves handy at snaking cable around the offices.

"They'd show you what they were doing on the computer," said Mr. Gustin's wife, Patsy, referring to the Web page designs. "They never were secretive. They always had the doors open."

When the group left, Mr. Gustin said, they said that they had been called to California and that their superior had been afraid they would get snowed in at their retreat. They said they hoped to come back in the spring, he said, but never did.

The Gustins said the group members had never mentioned anything about religion or the occult. And at the grocery store near Manzano, Josephine Castillo said she thought the group had left because the area was so pervasively Catholic that they could not hope to proselytize successfully.

But Mr. Thorsen, 68, the current owner of the compound, has told The Tribune that he discussed the group's beliefs with them and that they tried to recruit him and his wife to accompany them to California. They even sent videotapes and cult writings from California.

Mr. Thorsen, who was not at the compound today, told The Tribune that he was active in New Mexico paramilitary groups and agreed with some of the ideas of the cult.

"They could see there was great oppression coming against the religious people of our nation," he told The Tribune. "There has been great falling away and persecution." But other ideas he could not accept, he said, in particular their concept that Jesus was an extraterrestrial being.

Former Cultists Warn of Believers Now Adrift

BY JAMES BROOKE | APRIL 2, 1997

THE MASS SUICIDE of followers of the Heaven's Gate cult left many other believers spiritually adrift across the United States and Canada, say two former cult members who talk frequently to followers.

Although San Diego law-enforcement authorities said this week that they had "no indication" that there were any believers beyond the 39 who committed suicide in Rancho Santa Fe, Calif., the two former members said they had maintained regular contact with followers around the country.

Sharon K. Walsh, the first recruit of cult founders Marshall Herff Applewhite and Bonnie Lu Nettles, said her mother, her stepfather and a niece are among the followers who still prepare for the golden day when a U.F.O. will land on earth to take them to heaven. On Monday, California authorities confirmed that Mrs. Walsh's half-sister, Judith Ann Rowland, was among those who committed suicide.

"There are probably as many as 50 followers left," estimated Mrs. Walsh, a no-nonsense 53-year-old stockbroker who spent the summer of 1974 proselytizing with the cult's founders.

Another former cult member, Aaron Greenberg of Eugene, Ore., estimated today that surviving Heaven's Gate believers numbered in the hundreds.

"I personally know about 60 to 80, but I feel there are hundreds," said Mr. Greenberg, who keeps up with followers through a loose telephone network. "There are about 1,000 people who passed through this thing."

Mr. Greenberg said that on Monday he talked by telephone with one man in Canada, who is part of a group of 40 believers, and with another man in New York, who is part of a group of 60. Both men, Mr. Greenberg said, told him that the cult followers, who meet periodically, were converging this week on a secret site in the Southwest.

"This is not a good thing," warned Mr. Greenberg, who left the group in 1976 after six months. Referring to the cultists' farewell videotape, widely aired on television in recent days, Mr. Greenberg added: "Remember what they say in the videotapes: 'Come join us, the time is now, the window is small.' "

Mrs. Walsh thinks that her mother and stepfather, both 78 years old, "wanted to go, but were probably turned down because Herff wanted 39."

She speculated that for Mr. Applewhite, a former seminarian who had studied numerology, the number 39 may have had special significance because 3 plus 9 equals 12 — the number of Christ's disciples.

Mrs. Walsh recalled the training undertaken by her mother and stepfather, whom she would identify only as a Midwest farm couple whose first names are Lorraine and Floyd.

"They had drills where they had to be ready to go in 12 minutes," she said. "They actually would run out of the house into a field. They thought they would be beamed up."

In this affluent southern suburb of Denver, Mrs. Walsh sat in her living room Monday night with her husband, Jim, and reviewed 16 months of letters she received from Mr. Applewhite and Ms. Nettles from February 1973 to May 1974, the month she left her first husband and two young daughters to join the pair's proselytizing work. The cult leaders, believing they had a divine mission to illuminate humanity, sometimes signed their letters "Two Lampstands" or "Two Candlesticks."

The letters to Mrs. Walsh, whom the founders called the "first disciple," provide rare insight into the early thinking and way of life of the wandering pair, who later preached under the names Bo and Peep, Guinea and Pig, and Do and Ti.

Closing their astrological bookstore in Houston on Jan. 2, 1974, the two embarked on an 18-month road trip that crisscrossed the United States and Canada, from south to north and east to west.

"I provided their main means of support," recalled Mrs. Walsh, who faults herself for introducing the pair to her mother. A housewife at the time, she mailed them family heirlooms — a 1790 Bible and a turn-of-the-century postcard collection — so they could sell the items to get gas money. In addition, members of Mrs. Walsh's Hatha Yoga group sent money to Ms. Nettles, a longtime Houston psychic, in return for personalized astrological charts.

The letters from Ms. Nettles and Mr. Applewhite describe camping in state parks, bathing in frigid streams, washing clothes in coin-operated laundries and receiving mail at general delivery windows of big city post offices. The pair moved quickly, leaving no traces.

"Please be discreet as to our whereabouts," implored one of the dozens of letters. When Mrs. Walsh later joined them on the road, she discovered why: Mr. Applewhite had stolen a rental car in St. Louis in December 1973, and the pair routinely ran out on motel bills.

"They said at first they slept in camps or roadside parks in their car, until one day Our Father revealed to them a part of the scripture in which Jesus said the 'Lord will be as a thief in the night,' " Mrs. Walsh wrote in a manuscript she is preparing about her three months with the pair. "They checked into a motel giving a fictitious name. They took all meals at the motel charging it to their bill, and then left very early on the morning of their departure, without paying."

The use of Mrs. Walsh's gasoline credit card was their undoing. After she left her first husband with a family car, he filed a complaint that led to Mr. Applewhite's arrest in Aug. 28, 1974.

"According to my gas tickets, they'd be on the West Coast, and then three days later, they'd be on the East Coast," her first husband, James Morgan, told The Houston Chronicle in 1975. "They may try to tell people they get around some other way. But I've got proof they're not doing any of this astro traveling."

Mrs. Walsh broke with the pair, briefly reconciled with her husband, and he dropped the charges. But Mr. Applewhite spent four months in jail in St. Louis for stealing the rental car.

On the road, the missionary pair failed to make recruits. In their letters, they complained that their modern-day prophecies were falling on deaf ears.

"He would be branded a fanatic and nut too if He came today like He did then," Ms. Nettles wrote of Jesus on Aug. 27, 1973. "Whenever anyone calls you a witch or implies insanity, feel thankful — you will get to a state where you will feel in the world, but not part of it."

"By social, psychiatric, medical & religious standards we and you have long since lost our sanity," Mr. Applewhite wrote on the same day. "If you think that '2 religious fanatics' — '2 Candlesticks' — find any religious or worldly pleasure in their mission — just put yourself in our shoes and imagine what we're up against."

Although the letters make no mention of U.F.O.'s, the pair seemed to be traveling intellectually in that direction.

"We are becoming increasingly awkward in this world's structure and giggle a lot at ourselves as two folks from outerspace would as they realize they can't fit the patterns of social practice," reads a November 1973 letter, signed "Much Love, Herff."

"When we converse in our minds (while thinking) we are really listening to the conversations between the alien spirits," reads a letter from the pair, dated Feb. 27, 1974.

In that letter, the pair already refer to their bodies as "vehicles" or "houses" that must eventually be shed to reach a higher level, a Christian concept that Mr. Applewhite apparently distorted last week when he led his followers into suicide.

These themes recur in an unpublished manuscript that Mr. Applewhite and Ms. Nettles wrote in January 1973, with the title: "I Can't Believe That — But You Must."

"Deaths, marriage, sweethearts, and even newborn babes are elements which keep us from climbing out of the physical," wrote the pair, who later pressed followers to turn their backs on friends, family and fortune.

In a passage that foreshadowed events 25 years later, they wrote: "Man has experienced in space travel the process necessary to leave the earth magnet and arrive at a space which seems to be Nirvana, the absence of a gravity force."

Suicide Cult's Possessions Auctioned Off

BY THE NEW YORK TIMES | NOV. 22, 1999

MANY OF THE ITEMS on the block were ordinary enough — a plastic laundry hamper, card tables, camping gear, clothes, tools, cookbooks, a sewing machine. Only a few — a voluminous collection of books about U.F.O.'s, 20 metal-frame bunk beds, a pair of black Nike sneakers — offered a hint of their macabre origins.

The items auctioned by county officials today were the last earthly possessions of the 39 members of the Heaven's Gate cult who killed themselves nearly three years ago, in hopes of boarding a spaceship that they believed was trailing the Hale-Bopp comet. The mass suicide was one of the worst in United States history.

The belongings on sale today offered no insight into what led their former owners to a point in life where they believed the path to the heavens began with a lethal mix of barbiturates, vodka and apple sauce. There were 183 lots in all, which also included television sets, videocassette recorders, a camcorder and three cars.

About 375 people came to bid on the items with a mix of gallows humor, indifference and ignorance. Their reasons for bidding included basic need, morbid curiosity and commercial intent.

"I've got to go; this is not for me," said David Sauceda, a 40-year-old construction worker who was looking for tools when he was told the source of the items.

The curators of the Museum of Death, which is expected to open in Hollywood in January, bought a bunk-bed frame to be used in a display about cult deaths.

Ken Powell, 34, and his wife, Laura, 29, bought seven bunk beds that they said they intended to sell for a profit on the Internet.

"They might go for a couple grand each," Mr. Powell said. "You don't know. There are some weird people out there."

The bodies of the cult members were discovered on March 26, 1997, in a seven-bedroom house in an affluent suburb, after the cult's leader, Marshall Herff Applewhite, had sent several people a videotape in which he said the members would be "shedding their containers" and "leaving this planet." A videotape of the scene made by investigators from the Sheriff's Department showed the cult members uniformly dressed in black track suits and black Nike sneakers, covered with purple shrouds.

The auction was delayed by a probate battle involving two former members of the group, Mark and Sarah King, who wanted control of the estate. Though they ultimately lost, the county agreed to sell them the "intellectual property" in the estate — manuscripts, artwork, computers and the like, as well as patches bearing the cult's logo — for $2,000. Kent W. Schirmer, the chief of San Diego County's property division, said the Kings wanted to keep the materials out of the public realm.

Proceeds from the auction will be given to families of the dead to cover the cost of burial. Mr. Schirmer said that the crowd was not much larger than it is for most such auctions and that the bidding amounts were average. By the end of the day the items had fetched nearly $33,000.

Bidding was heaviest on the books and on the bunk-bed frames, which generally sold for $110 to $130.

Few in the crowd of bidders shared the cult's beliefs or acknowledged a fascination with death. A man and woman dressed completely in black and gray determinedly bid several hundred dollars for most, if not all, of the books in the estate, but would not speak with reporters afterward.

Julie Stangeland, a collectibles trader who holds a certificate in mortuary science, said she bought one of the bed frames because she was fascinated by cults and the power their leaders exert over members. But she added: "I don't want to sound morbid because I'm really not. If God would alter the universe so people could live forever, I'd be kicking my heels up."

Edward C. Songer, 66, a federal telecommunications worker, said he bid on boxes of crimping tools, wires and phone cards because he was able to pay $60 for items that would normally cost about $200.

"It's just for my occupation; it's for my life," Mr. Songer said. "It doesn't bother me where they came from."

Some voiced discomfort with the origin of the items.

Mike Benavides, 25, said he wanted to buy a VCR, because his had broken down, and maybe another piece of memorabilia as well. But his wife, Jennifer, 21, said she was unsure whether she would allow something like that in the house.

Most people said they bid in the hopes of owning a novel, if grim, piece of Americana.

"It's an odd piece of San Diego history, but it happened here nonetheless," said Andrew Shaw, a 27-year-old college student who also bought a bed frame. He said he would put it in his guest bedroom.

But would he sleep on it? "Absolutely not," he said.

CHAPTER 5

Keith Raniere: Nxivm

In 1998, Keith Raniere founded Nxivm, a multi-level marketing company offering personal and professional development seminars, mainly to the rich and relatively famous. Some female members, however, were persuaded by Raniere and his acolytes to make a much deeper commitment. These women joined a secret sorority. They were branded with Raniere's initials, and served as his sexual partners, source of income and labor pool. Raniere was arrested in March 2018 for sex trafficking and forced labor, and Nxivm shut down two months later.

Inside a Secretive Group Where Women Are Branded

BY BARRY MEIER | OCT. 17, 2017

ALBANY — Last March, five women gathered in a home near here to enter a secret sisterhood they were told was created to empower women.

To gain admission, they were required to give their recruiter — or "master," as she was called — naked photographs or other compromising material and were warned that such "collateral" might be publicly released if the group's existence were disclosed.

The women, in their 30s and 40s, belonged to a self-help organization called Nxivm, which is based in Albany and has chapters across the country, Canada and Mexico.

Sarah Edmondson, one of the participants, said she had been told she would get a small tattoo as part of the initiation. But she was not prepared for what came next.

Each woman was told to undress and lie on a massage table, while three others restrained her legs and shoulders. According to one of them, their "master," a top Nxivm official named Lauren Salzman, instructed them to say: "Master, please brand me, it would be an honor."

A female doctor proceeded to use a cauterizing device to sear a 2-inch-square symbol below each woman's hip, a procedure that took 20 to 30 minutes. For hours, muffled screams and the smell of burning tissue filled the room.

"I wept the whole time," Ms. Edmondson recalled. "I disassociated out of my body."

Since the late 1990s, an estimated 16,000 people have enrolled in courses offered by Nxivm (pronounced Nex-e-um), which it says are designed to bring about greater self-fulfillment by eliminating psychological and emotional barriers. Most participants take some workshops, like the group's "Executive Success Programs," and resume their lives. But other people have become drawn more deeply into Nxivm, giving up careers, friends and families to become followers of its leader, Keith Raniere, who is known within the group as "Vanguard."

Both Nxivm and Raniere, 57, have long attracted controversy. Former members have depicted him as a man who manipulated his adherents, had sex with them and urged women to follow near-starvation diets to achieve the type of physique he found appealing.

Now, as talk about the secret sisterhood and branding has circulated within Nxivm, scores of members are leaving. Interviews with a dozen of them portray a group spinning more deeply into disturbing practices. Many members said they feared that confessions about indiscretions would be used to blackmail them.

Mark Vicente, a filmmaker and former top Nxivm official, said that after hearing about the secret society, he confronted Raniere.

"I said 'whatever you are doing, you are heading for a blowup,' " Mr. Vicente said.

Several former members have asked state authorities to investigate the group's practices, but officials have declined to pursue action.

In July, Ms. Edmondson filed a complaint with the New York State Department of Health against Danielle Roberts, a licensed osteopath and follower of Raniere, who performed the branding, according to Ms. Edmondson and another woman. In a letter, the agency said it would not look into Roberts because she was not acting as Ms. Edmondson's doctor when the branding is said to have happened.

Separately, a state police investigator told Ms. Edmondson and two other women that officials would not pursue their criminal complaint against Nxivm because their actions had been consensual, a text message shows.

State medical regulators also declined to act on a complaint filed against another Nxivm-affilated physician, Brandon Porter. Porter, as part of an "experiment," showed women graphically violent film clips while a brain-wave machine and video camera recorded their reactions, according to two women who took part.

The women said they were not warned that some of the clips were violent, including footage of four women being murdered and dismembered.

"Please look into this ASAP," a former Nxivm member, Jennifer Kobelt, stated in her complaint. "This man needs to be stopped."

In September, regulators told Kobelt they concluded that the allegations against Porter did not meet the agency's definition of "medical misconduct," their letter shows.

Raniere and other top Nxivm officials, including Lauren Salzman, did not respond to repeated emails, letters or text messages seeking comment. Roberts and Porter also did not respond to inquiries.

Former members said that, inside Nxivm, they are being portrayed as defectors who want to destroy the group.

It is not clear how many women were branded or which Nxivm officials were aware of the practice.

A copy of a text message Raniere sent to a female follower indicates that he knew women were being branded and that the symbol's design incorporated his initials.

"Not initially intended as my initials but they rearranged it slightly for tribute," Raniere wrote, ("if it were abraham lincolns or bill gates initials no one would care.)"

JOINING THE SISTERHOOD

Ms. Edmondson, who lives in Vancouver and helped start Nxivm's chapter there, was thrilled when Lauren Salzman arrived in January to teach workshops.

The women, both in their early 40s, were close and Ms. Edmondson regarded Ms. Salzman as a confidante and mentor.

"Lauren was someone I really looked up to as a rock star within the company," said Ms. Edmondson, an actress who joined Nxivm about a decade ago.

During her visit, Ms. Salzman said she had something "really amazing" she wanted to share. "It is kind of strange and top secret and in order for me to tell you about it you need to give me something as collateral to make sure you don't speak about it," Ms. Edmondson recalled her saying.

The proposition seemed like a test of trust. After Ms. Edmondson wrote a letter detailing past indiscretions, Ms. Salzman told her about the secret sorority.

She said it had been formed as a force for good, one that could grow into a network that could influence events like elections. To become effective, members had to overcome weaknesses that Raniere taught were common to women — an overemotional nature, a failure to keep promises and an embrace of the role of victim, according to Ms. Edmondson and other members.

Submission and obedience would be used as tools to achieve those goals, several women said. The sisterhood would comprise circles, each led by a "master" who would recruit six "slaves," according to two women. In time, they would recruit slaves of their own.

"She made it sound like a bad-ass bitch boot camp," Ms. Edmondson said.

Ms. Edmondson and others said that during training, the women were required to send their master texts that read "Morning M" and "Night M." During drills, a master texted her slaves "?" and they had 60 seconds to reply "Ready M."

Trainees who failed had to pay penalties, including fasting, or could face physical punishments, two women said.

In March, Ms. Edmondson arrived for an initiation ceremony at Ms. Salzman's home in Clifton Park, New York, a town about 20 miles north of Albany where Raniere and some followers live. After undressing, she was led to a candlelit ceremony, where she removed a blindfold and saw Ms. Salzman's other slaves for the first time. The women were then driven to a nearby house, where the branding took place.

In the spring, the sorority grew as women joined different circles. Slaves added compromising collateral every month to Dropbox accounts and a Google Document was used to list a timetable for recruiting new slaves, several women said.

Around the same time, an actress, Catherine Oxenberg, said she learned her daughter had been initiated into the sorority.

"I felt sick to my stomach," said Ms. Oxenberg, who starred in the 1980s television series "Dynasty."

Ms. Oxenberg had become increasingly concerned about her 26-year-old daughter, India, who looked emaciated from dieting. She told her mother she had not had a menstrual period for a year and that her hair was falling out.

Ms. Oxenberg said she invited her daughter home in late May to try to get her away from the group.

When Ms. Oxenberg confronted her about the sorority, her daughter defended its practices.

"She said it was a character-building experience," Ms. Oxenberg said.

'HUMANS CAN BE NOBLE'

By the time the secret group was taking shape, Mark Vicente, the filmmaker, had been a faithful follower of Mr. Raniere for more than a decade.

Mr. Vicente said he had been contacted by Ms. Salzman's mother, Nancy, a co-founder of Nxivm who is known as "Prefect," after the 2004 release of a documentary he co-directed that explored spirituality and physics.

Soon, Mr. Vicente was taking courses that he said helped him expose his fears and learn strategies that made him feel more resolute.

He also made a documentary called "Encender el Corazón," or "Ignite the Heart," which lionized Mr. Raniere's work in Mexico.

"Keith Raniere is an activist, scientist, philosopher and, above all, humanitarian," Mr. Vicente says in the film.

Mr. Raniere has used those words to describe himself. On his website, he said he spoke in full sentences by age 1, mastered high school mathematics by 12 and taught himself to play "concert level" piano. At 16, he entered Rensselaer Polytechnic Institute in Troy, N.Y.

Before Nxivm, he helped run a company called Consumers' Buyline Inc., which offered discounts to members on groceries and other products.

In the mid-1990s, several state attorneys general investigated it as a suspected pyramid scheme; Mr. Raniere and his associates agreed to shut it down.

Through Nxivm, Mr. Raniere transformed himself into a New Age teacher with long hair and a guru-like manner of speaking.

"Humans can be noble," he says on his website. "The question is: will we put forth what is necessary?"

By many accounts, Mr. Raniere sleeps during the day and goes out at night to play volleyball or take female followers for long walks. Several women described him as warm, funny and eager to talk about subjects that interested them.

Others saw a different side. Nxivm sued several former members, accusing them of stealing its trade secrets, among other things.

Mr. Vicente said he was aware of the negative publicity, including a 2012 series by The Albany Times-Union that described alleged abuses inside Nxivm.

Mr. Vicente's views began to change this year after his wife was ostracized when she left Nxivm and he heard rumors about the secret sorority.

Mr. Vicente said he got evasive answers when he asked Mr. Raniere about the group. Mr. Raniere acknowledged giving "five women permission to do something," but did not elaborate, other than to say he would investigate, Mr. Vicente said.

Mr. Vicente said he suspected Mr. Raniere was lying to him and may have done so before. Suddenly, self-awareness techniques he had learned felt like tools that had been used to control him.

"No one goes in looking to have their personality stripped away," he said. "You just don't realize what is happening."

FOLLOWERS START TO FLEE

In May, Sarah Edmondson began to recoil from her embrace of the secret society.

Her husband, Anthony Ames, who was also a Nxivm member, learned about her branding and the couple both wanted out.

Before quitting, Mr. Ames went to Nxivm's offices in Albany to collect money he said the group owed him.

He had his cellphone in his pocket and turned on its recorder.

On the recording, Mr. Ames tells another member that Ms. Edmondson was branded and that other women told him about handing over collateral. "This is criminal," Mr. Ames says.

The voice of a woman — who Ames said is Lauren Salzman — is heard trying to calm him. "I don't think you are open to having a conversation," she said.

"You are absolutely right, I'm not open to having a conversation," he replied. "My wife got branded."

A few days later, many of Mr. Raniere's followers learned of the secret society from a website run by a Buffalo-area businessman, Frank R. Parlato Jr. Mr. Parlato had been locked in a long legal battle with two sisters, Sara and Clare Bronfman, who are members of Nxivm and the daughters of Edgar Bronfman, the deceased chairman of Seagram Company.

In 2011, the Bronfman sisters sued Mr. Parlato, whom they had hired as a consultant, alleging he had defrauded them of $1 million.

Four years later, in 2015, the Justice Department indicted him on charges of fraud and other crimes arising from alleged activities, including defrauding the Bronfmans. Mr. Parlato has denied the claims and the case is pending.

Mr. Parlato started a website, The Frank Report, which he uses to lambaste prosecutors, Mr. Raniere and the Bronfmans. In early June, Mr. Parlato published the first in a torrent of salacious posts under the headline, “Branded Slaves and Master Raniere.”

A Nxivm follower, Soukaina Mehdaoui, said she reached out to Mr. Raniere after reading the post. Ms. Mehdaoui, 25, was a newcomer to Nxivm but the two had grown close.

She said Mr. Raniere told her the secret sorority began after three women offered damaging collateral to seal lifetime vows of obedience to him.

While Ms. Mehdaoui had joined the sorority, the women in her circle were not branded. She was appalled.

“There are things I didn’t know that I didn’t sign up for, and I’m not even hearing about it from you,” she texted Mr. Raniere.

Mr. Raniere texted back about his initials and the brand.

By then, panic was spreading inside Nxivm. Slaves were ordered to delete encrypted messages between them and erase Google documents, two women said. To those considering breaking away, it was not clear whom they could trust and who were Nxivm loyalists.

Late one night, Ms. Mehdaoui met secretly with another Nxivm member. They took out their cellphones to show they were not recording the conversation.

Both decided to leave Nxivm, despite concerns that the group would retaliate by releasing their "collateral" or suing them.

Ms. Mehdaoui said that when she went to say goodbye to Mr. Raniere, he urged her to stay.

"Do you think, I'm bad, I don't agree with abuses," she recalled him saying. He said the group "gives women tools to be powerful, to regain their power for the sake of building love."

Nxivm recently filed criminal complaints with the Vancouver police against Ms. Edmondson and two other women accusing them of mischief and other crimes in connection with the firm's now-closed center there, according to Ms. Edmondson. The women have denied the allegations. A spokesman for the Vancouver police declined to comment.

Ms. Edmondson and other former followers of Mr. Raniere said they were focusing on recovering.

"There is no playbook for leaving a cult," she said.

SUSAN C. BEACHY contributed research.

Federal Officials Reportedly Investigating Group Where Women Were Branded

BY BARRY MEIER AND PAULINA VILLEGAS | DEC. 21, 2017

THE JUSTICE DEPARTMENT has started an investigation into a self-described self-help group in which women were branded with a symbol containing its leader's initials, several people contacted as part of the inquiry said.

Those people said that agents with the FBI had recently contacted or questioned them about the group, which is called Nxivm. They spoke on the condition of anonymity because officials asked them not to discuss the inquiry, which appears to be at an early stage.

In a related move, Gov. Andrew M. Cuomo of New York is expected to soon recommend possible changes in how state regulators review complaints against doctors, a spokesman said. The decision follows the disclosure that health department officials declined to act on complaints about two doctors affiliated with Nxivm, including one who reportedly used a surgical device to brand women. Inquiries into those two doctors are now underway, a spokesman for the governor said.

John Marzulli, a spokesman for the office of the U.S. attorney for the Eastern District of New York, which is reportedly leading the inquiry, said he could neither confirm nor deny whether an investigation into Nxivm, which is based in Albany, was underway.

The developments follow an October article in The New York Times that disclosed how some women who joined a secret sorority within Nxivm were branded with a symbol that incorporated the initials of the group's leader, Keith Raniere.

Women were also told that compromising information they had provided to join the sorority, such as naked photographs, would be publicly released if they disclosed its existence. The sorority revolved around "master-slave" relationships, former Nxivm members said, in

NATHANIEL BROOKS/THE NEW YORK TIMES

The offices of the Nxivm Executive Success Program in Albany, N.Y.

which women faced punishments, including physical ones, for not following a master's order.

Since the late 1990s, over 16,000 people have enrolled in courses offered by Nxivm (pronounced Nex-e-um), which the group says are designed to bring about greater self-fulfillment by eliminating psychological and emotional barriers.

Most participants take some workshops, like the group's Executive Success Programs, and resume their lives. But other people have become drawn more deeply into Nxivm, giving up careers, friends and families to become devoted followers of Mr. Raniere. Critics and former members have described the group's practices as cultlike.

Mr. Raniere, whose followers refer to him as "Vanguard," urges women to follow near-starvation diets of 500 to 800 calories a day to achieve the body shape he finds appealing. Some women who have followed that diet have stopped menstruating and lost hair, according to former Nxivm members.

Mr. Raniere, 57, recently left the Albany area and traveled to Mexico, where Nxivm has hundreds of followers, to stay with an adherent in Monterrey. Former associates said Mr. Raniere had never previously gone to Mexico. A former Nxivm member in Mexico said that Mr. Raniere was seen recently in Monterrey, though his current whereabouts is not known.

Mr. Raniere and other Nxivm officials did not respond to requests for interviews or repeated emails. A lawyer who represents the group, Robert D. Crockett, also did not respond to written questions, including whether federal or state officials had contacted Nxivm.

In recent weeks, Nxivm's leaders have posted statements on the website of Executive Success Programs, contending that the secret sorority was not connected to Nxivm and that Mr. Raniere was unaware of its practices.

Nxivm also stated that it has conducted an independent investigation of the sorority and determined that the women in it are healthy and happy.

"Our experts, a forensic psychiatrist of international repute, psychologists and ex-law enforcement say members of the sorority are thriving, healthy, happy, better off and haven't been coerced," Mr. Raniere said in a statement. The group did not name the experts.

Several former Nxivm members said that senior women in the group, including the daughter of its co-founder, were involved in the sorority and branding ceremonies. In addition, a text message sent by Mr. Raniere indicated that he was aware that women were being branded with a symbol that contained his initials.

"Not initially intended as my initials but they rearranged it slightly for tribute," he wrote in that message. "(if it were abraham lincolns or bill gates initials no one would care.)"

Nxivm did not respond to requests for the report of its independent investigation or the names of the experts involved. But an actress, Catherine Oxenberg, said a well-known forensic psychiatrist, Dr. Park Dietz, recently contacted her and said that Nxivm had hired him to evaluate her 26-year-old daughter, India Oxenberg.

In May, another doctor who examined Ms. Oxenberg's daughter told her that the severe diet she was following had jeopardized her ability to have children. Ms. Oxenberg has tried without success to convince her daughter, who has followed Mr. Raniere for years, to leave Nxivm.

In response to written questions, Dr. Dietz said he has examined only one female participant in Nxivm, though he declined, citing issues of patient confidentiality, to confirm that it was Ms. Oxenberg.

He added that his initial examination of the woman had not found evidence of "brainwashing" and that she appeared "happy," though troubled by what she described as false media reports about the group.

Dr. Dietz said that Nxivm had not hired him to examine matters related to the secret sorority, stating it was his understanding that the group "is not a Nxivm entity but rather a private sorority of women."

In recent months, Nxivm has also attempted to hire lobbyists in Albany to represent it before politicians and regulators there. It has also sued or sought to bring criminal charges against former members.

For example, the Mexican branch of Nxivm recently sued a former member there who quit the organization after 13 years upon hearing about the secret sorority and the branding.

The man, Toni Zarattini, said that when he asked other Nxivm members in Mexico about those practices he was told to stop doing so. "There is no problem here, all is good, don't ask more questions and don't say a word to anyone else," Mr. Zarattini said he was told.

Nxivm's Mexican affiliate is headed by Emiliano Salinas, a son of that country's former president. Its ranks include members of Mexico's ruling elite, including a daughter of the publisher of one of the country's biggest newspapers, Reforma. Several women who belong to the group in Mexico have traveled to Albany, where they were branded, two former Nxivm members said.

Asked about the practice, Mr. Salinas reiterated that the sorority was not affiliated with Nxivm and added that it was important to "respect the decisions" members make in their private lives.

He added the company had sued Mr. Zarattini because he and others had tried to extort Nxivm by asking for money in exchange for not revealing information, an assertion Mr. Zarattini has denied.

Earlier this month, a Mexican judge dismissed the lawsuit against Mr. Zarattini, saying it was based on inadequate evidence. A lawyer for Nxivm said the group has another action pending against him, but lawyers for Mr. Zarattini said they were unaware of it.

His friends "are in some ways kidnapped; their minds, their emotions have been taken for ransom," said Mr. Zarattini, who was kidnapped and brutalized a decade ago by a drug cartel. "I can't allow these secrets to keep going because that contributes in some way to that."

WILLIAM K. RASHBAUM contributed reporting.

Charges Filed Against Leader of Secretive Group Where Women Were Branded

BY BARRY MEIER | MARCH 26, 2018

FEDERAL AUTHORITIES CHARGED the head of an Albany-area group with forcing women to engage in sex, according to a complaint unsealed Monday.

The man, Keith Raniere, was arrested by federal officials in Mexico, where he has lived for the past five months, one federal official said. Mr. Raniere, who faces sex trafficking and related charges, was scheduled to appear Tuesday at a hearing in Texas.

According to the complaint, female followers of the group headed by Mr. Raniere were forced to have sex with him because they feared that if they did not do so, compromising material they had provided about themselves would be released publicly.

For two decades, Mr. Raniere has served as the leader of an organization near Albany called Nxivm (pronounced Nex-e-um). The group, which describes itself as a "self-help" organization, denies it is a cult. But former members have said that Mr. Raniere demands obedience from his followers, who refer to him as "Vanguard."

Mr. Raniere left the United States for Mexico shortly after The New York Times published an article in October that detailed how women who belonged to a secret sorority within Nxivm were branded by a doctor who used a cauterizing device to sear a symbol into their lower abdomens.

To gain admission to the sorority, women were required to give their recruiter — or "master," as she was called — naked photographs or other compromising material and were warned that such "collateral" might be publicly released if the group's existence were disclosed.

Mr. Raniere denied knowing about the branding, and Nxivm contended in a statement that women participating in the secret sorority

BRENDAN MCDERMID/REUTERS/NEWSCOM

Attorneys representing Nxivm leader Keith Raniere, Marc Agnifilo, left, and Paul DerOhannesian.

were happy and thriving. But an email obtained by The Times showed that Mr. Raniere wrote a female follower that the design of the symbol used to brand women incorporated his initials as a "tribute" to him.

"Not initially intended as my initials but they rearranged it slightly for tribute," Mr. Raniere wrote in that email, "(if it were abraham lincolns or bill gates initials no one would care.)"

Shortly after the publication of the Times article, the U.S. Attorney's Office in Brooklyn opened an investigation into Nxivm. New York state officials are also investigating the group.

In an affidavit filed as part of the complaint, an agent with the FBI, Michael Lever, stated that his inquiry had determined that Mr. Raniere maintained a "rotating group of fifteen to twenty women" with whom he maintained sexual relations. Those women were allowed to have sex only with him, the agent stated in the filing.

Women who joined the secret sorority were unaware that Mr.

Raniere was its supreme master, Mr. Lever said. And some slaves were required by their masters, who included high-ranking women within Nxivm, "to have sex with Mr. Raniere, which they then did," the filing said.

Mr. Lever said two women who cooperated with the federal investigation said they believed they had to "complete the assignment or risk release of their collateral."

When one of the women started having sex with Mr. Raniere, he began giving her money and provided a job, but when she defected he demanded the money back, according to the filing.

Both Nxivm and Mr. Raniere have long attracted controversy. Former members have depicted him as a man who manipulated his adherents, had sex with them and urged women to follow near-starvation diets to achieve the type of physique he found appealing.

Over the years, much of Nxivm's funding has come from Clare and Sara Bronfman, sisters who are members of the group and the youngest daughters of Edgar Bronfman, the chairman of the Seagram Co. who died in 2013.

A lawyer who has represented Nxivm could not immediately be reached for comment.

At the Texas hearing on Tuesday, prosecutors plan to argue for Mr. Raniere to remain in custody while he is sent back to Brooklyn to face charges.

In an eight-page memo, prosecutors argued that Mr. Raniere "has a long-history of systematically exploiting women through coercive practices for his own financial and sexual benefit."

Prosecutors said that Mr. Raniere, while pretending to be penniless, "has spent his life profiting from pyramid schemes and has otherwise received financial backing from independently wealthy women" like the Bronfman sisters.

They also asserted that Mr. Raniere and the mother of his child had taken hundreds of thousands of dollars from a bank account that "contains over $8 million" and is in the name of one of his deceased lovers.

Authorities Raid Homes Linked to Cultlike Group That Branded Women

BY BARRY MEIER | MARCH 27, 2018

FEDERAL AUTHORITIES RAIDED two homes near Albany that were associated with a cultlike group called Nxivm, in which women were branded with a symbol that contained its leader's initials, according to media reports.

The raids followed the arrest Sunday of Nxivm's leader, Keith Raniere, on charges that he forced female followers to have sex with him. Mr. Raniere, who is known to his followers as "Vanguard," is expected to be arraigned in Federal District Court in Brooklyn on sex-trafficking charges.

One of the raids on Tuesday took place in Half Moon, N.Y., at the home of a former psychiatric nurse, Nancy Salzman, who founded Nxivm (pronounced Nex-ee-um) along with Mr. Raniere, according to news reports. Another area home was also raided.

Nxivm denies it is a cult, and has described itself as a "self-help" organization. But former members have said that Mr. Raniere demands cultlike obedience from followers.

Authorities began investigating Nxivm after The New York Times published an article in October detailing how women who belonged to a secret sorority within Nxivm were branded by a doctor who used a cauterizing device to sear a symbol into their lower abdomens.

To gain admission to the sorority, women were required to give their recruiter naked photographs or other compromising material and were warned that such "collateral" might be publicly released if the group's existence were disclosed.

Federal authorities described Mr. Raniere, 57, as the ultimate master of the sorority and charged that woman were forced to have sex with him because they feared that their collateral would be released if they did not.

Reports about the raids were broadcast or published by several Albany outlets including News 10, an ABC affiliate, and a newspaper, the Albany Times Union.

Ms. Salzman could not be reached for comment.

Inside Nxivm, the 'Sex Cult' That Preached Empowerment

BY VANESSA GRIGORIADIS | MAY 29, 2018

Why did female members follow a guru named Keith Raniere, who now stands accused of sex trafficking? He made them feel like they were in control.

ONE WINTER MORNING in a conventional suburb outside Albany, N.Y., Nancy Salzman, the 63-year-old president of a self-improvement company named Nxivm, sat on a mahogany-colored stool in her kitchen. Her tasteful home was surrounded by other Nxivm members' modest townhouses or capacious stone mansions that seemed to spring up out of nowhere, like mushrooms, on the suburban streets. In Salzman's den, a photo of her with her two adult daughters hung on a wall, the three of them wearing smiles as wide as ancient Greek masks of comedy; the same happy photo served as the wallpaper on Salzman's laptop. A hairless Sphynx cat prowled the lovely buffet of croissants and fruit on her kitchen island.

Salzman, an extremely fit woman wearing the type of thin athleisure sweatshirt that's all the rage with the middle-aged bourgeoisie these days, turned her attention to a woman sitting at the island: Jacqueline, a 27-year-old psychology student with long dark hair, who told me that she hadn't experienced anything as effective as Nxivm (pronounced "nexium," like the heartburn medication). Like Scientology's L. Ron Hubbard, whose 1950 handbook "Dianetics" was billed as the "modern science of mental health" and whose pseudoscientific methods were, in his view, world-changing, Keith Raniere, Nxivm's 57-year-old founder, believed his organization could heal individuals and transform the world. The way Nxivm did this was through techniques, or "technology," meant to rewire your emotional self.

Salzman, who has training in neurolinguistic programming, which involves hypnosis and techniques of mirroring another individual to create deep rapport, was about to embark on a therapy session in which she would ask Jacqueline to cast her mind back to her childhood, as Nxivm sessions often do. Jacqueline had come to her with a phobia: She flips out when she gets on a plane. One time, she had to get off an airplane that had boarded because she became nervous, and when she wanted to get back on, the flight attendants wouldn't let her.

Salzman nodded. In a near whisper, she asked Jacqueline a stream of intimate questions not only about her fear of flying but also about her parents' relationship. She ascertained that Jacqueline believed her mother was ill used by her father, who forced the family to move often, by air. "It was always gray around her," Jacqueline said sadly, of her mother. "She had a horrible life." But at the same time, she said, her upbringing made her feel as if she always needed a man to protect her.

Listening to Salzman's questions, it became clear that she was positing that these issues — Jacqueline's fear of flying; her belief that her mother was forced into a terrible life by her father; and her inability to be an independent woman — were connected. We are controlling our own lives all the time, Salzman said. We are all in complete control. Jacqueline's mom had been in control but had chosen to be a victim. And Jacqueline was in control and had chosen to be a victim, too. "Are you pretending to be a helpless woman?" Salzman said earlier.

"That's the way I receive attention, that's kind of my thing," Jacqueline said.

"Women are allowed to be dependent on men," Salzman explained. "A great part of being a woman is no matter how you screw up your life, you can always move back in with your dad. Every time you have chosen to stay dependent, you have made a decision not to be independent." What if she became the person she relied on?

Within half an hour, Jacqueline had "upgraded" her belief system; closing her eyes, she said the tightness in her chest that she typically got when she thought about flying was gone. She also agreed to do one thing that terrified her each day for the next 30 days, and on a day when she indulged in a man's attention, she would do two terrifying things. Facing your fears, especially in conjunction with penance, was key to Nxivm. As Jacqueline prepared to leave, the two women hugged. "I don't know what happened," she said. "I feel really good."

THE SCENE IN SALZMAN'S HOME was intense but mostly cheery. Yet last October, The New York Times published an article reporting alarming practices by Nxivm. The article explained that some female members of the group, who called themselves "masters," had initiated other women, calling themselves "slaves," into a ritual of sisterhood at homes in and around Clifton Park, near Albany. First, they stripped naked. One by one, they lay on a massage table while a female osteopath, also a Nxivm member, used a cauterizing pen to brand the flesh near their pelvic bone. She carved a symbol that some women thought represented the four elements or the seven chakras or a horizontal bar with the Greek letters "alpha" and "mu," but if you squinted and looked again, contained within them a different talisman: a K and an R — Raniere's initials. Not all the women were told that these initials were present in the symbol.

Hundreds of members fled Nxivm after they learned about the branding, but much of the inner circle remained. Citing the fact that Raniere had a cast of girlfriends, the media declared that Nxivm was not a self-improvement company at all but rather a "sex-slave cult." A federal investigation was opened, culminating in Mexican police officers plucking Raniere from a pricey villa; he is now in a federal jail on the Brooklyn waterfront after being denied bail as a flight risk. Another Nxivm member, Allison Mack, a blond actress who played Clark Kent's friend on the long-running "Smallville," was arrested and later released on $5 million bail. Raniere and Mack were charged with sex trafficking and conspiracy to commit sex trafficking and forced labor. Federal agents also raided Salzman's home, seizing $523,000 in cash, some of it in shoe boxes. (She has not been charged with a crime to date.)

The group found itself under a microscope, its secrets exposed. Some members came from the highest reaches of society, forming a kind of heiress Illuminati. There were two daughters of Edgar Bronfman Sr.,

RUTH FREMSON/THE NEW YORK TIMES

Sarah Edmondson shows the brand she received as part of a secret sorority ritual while part of the self-help group Nxivm, in Vancouver, in 2017.

the former head of the Seagram Company; Pamela Cafritz, who died in 2016, the daughter of political donors Bill and Buffy Cafritz; a number of well-to-do Mexicans, including Emiliano Salinas, the son of the former Mexican president Carlos Salinas de Gortari, who has since publicly disavowed Raniere but remains affiliated with the group, and Rosa Laura Junco, the daughter of the president and chief executive of the newspaper publisher Grupo Reforma; as well as prominent TV genre actresses who discovered Nxivm on location in Vancouver, including Nicki Clyne from "Battlestar Galactica" and, of course, Mack.

These puzzle pieces formed the ultimate tabloid story in an age of the vast tabloidification of media, and a tale about female empowerment and lack thereof in a time of feminist uprising, laced with questions of consent and coercion wielded by a man of power without accountability. Some women were severely thin, possibly as a means of mind control. Key defectors began speaking out. "We were both upset," Sarah Edmondson, a former leader of Nxivm's Vancouver chapter, wrote by email recently about why she and her husband left after a decade in the organization. "And disgusted. About the brand and a lot more. Nothing was what we thought it was."

From inside the group, all this looked very different. "Come on, man, this sounds like a bad horror movie," a member named Eduardo Asunsolo told me incredulously about the recent media coverage. Since the group's founding in 1998, it has been a tightly knit organization, "like a family," as Raniere has described it. About 17,000 people have come through Nxivm's doors, though the number of those who have committed for life was far smaller, perhaps in the hundreds. (By comparison about 25,000 individuals in the United States are self-identified Scientologists.) Members believed that Raniere could heal them of emotional traumas, set them free from their fears and attachments, clear patterns of destructive thinking. Some believed he could heal them sexually too. "This is the white-collar spiritual path," an ex-member says. "You're on the monk's path, but you're not wearing a red robe with a shaved head."

Raniere presented himself as a great philosopher, an ethical man and a scientist pushing the bounds of human capability. He had not only devised classroom-based courses that lasted as long as 12 hours a day for 16 days — recalling the Landmark Forum, a self-development company that has its origins in the 1970s consciousness-raising seminar EST — but also advocated that his followers control habits of mind and body, like food and exercise. He also seemed to have a unique, pulsating idea that resonated with women, particularly wealthy ones. This was an intersection of theories about femininity, victimhood, money and ethics, much of it influenced by Ayn Rand, one of Raniere's favorite authors. The ultimate Nxivm member was "potent," in Nxian lingo — not only rich but emotionally disciplined, self-controlled, attractive, physically fit and slender — or, in the word most members themselves preferred, "badass."

Much of today's upper class is engaged in a frenzy of self-improvement. They want to be skinnier, healthier, younger-looking, smarter, nicer, more loving and, since Trump assumed the presidency, more politically aware too. But were they truly improving? They may eat more vegetables, but this age seems more narcissistic than any before, more beholden to snake oil, and has put many individuals in the grip of an uneasy self-image toggling between unrealistic grandiosity and soul-crushing envy. Nxivm positioned itself as the true self-improvement gospel.

As I observed in Salzman's kitchen, its core tenet was wildly optimistic. Members believed that humans can alter our emotional triggers and our beliefs about ourselves, particularly those formed in childhood. We don't need to be angry because our mothers withheld love; or selfish and self-protective because we were bullied in school; or fall in love with people who bestowed gifts upon us because we loved a grandmother who did. The unexamined among us allow these ancient self-perceptions to run the show in current time, but not Nxians. They "integrate" these experiences in intense, hypnotic, secret-telling sessions like the one I saw called Explorations of Meaning. In an E.M., you often "explore the meaning" of a memory and observe the misperception that has made it painful, thus reducing the power that the memory holds over you today. "It's the most potent way to deconstruct an emotional trigger" and permanently change the way you process it, a former member told me. Experiencing integration after integration, the Nxian feels light, buoyant and more powerful than before. "We are just trying to create joy," another member said.

Breaking down identity was only the first part of Nxivm — replacing your identity with another, or "replacing data with data," in Nxivm speak, was the second part. As Nxians erased their fears, they began doing what they truly wanted to do with their lives (or perhaps what Raniere or high-ranked members wanted them to do). I talked to a banker who remade himself as an actor. I talked to a diversity specialist at a Connecticut boarding school who decided she wanted to start a farm.

India Oxenberg, a daughter of the "Dynasty" actress Catherine Oxenberg, spoke to me about taking courses taught by the group in Los Angeles. She wanted to feel closer to her friends, boyfriend and family, whom she often felt like pushing away, whom she felt "not to use such a harsh word, but so repulsed by. Why can't I just be in the same room with my family who I love but at the same time I want to crawl out of my skin and run away?" After she took Nxivm courses, she said she realized that "I'm the one who is choosing to feel bad about the situation." She also decided that she didn't want to be in the entertainment business. She wanted to be a caterer.

Oxenberg moved to the Nxivm motherland, Clifton Park, to "focus on my growth." She signed up for the group's "university," which can reportedly cost $5,000 a month. Raniere's courses largely teach neurolinguistic programming techniques and introductory ethical and psychological theory, which students are encouraged to understand in the context of their own lives. Oxenberg took courses like Mobius, about healing the parts of yourself that you reject and not hating them in other people; and Human Pain, about understanding that love and pain often go together. Nxivm taught the power of penance as a time-tested shortcut to achieving self-improvement. Oxenberg took long walks alongside Raniere, her guru, to discuss her goals. He encouraged her to start her own business, and she did, calling her catering company Mix, because it was a mix of vegan, vegetarian and Mexican food. When she was done cooking, she delivered meals through suburban developments in a BMW.

Many members and ex-members of Nxivm that I spoke with — most of them fans of science and math, funny and strikingly perceptive — agreed on one thing: The "technology" worked. Raniere could program you. He had solved the equation of how to be a joyful human. Decide on your ethics and make them the guiding force in your life; do not make decisions that are not in line with those ethics. Look to create strength and character through discipline. Look to create love. Do not reject your family (unless your family rejects Nxivm, in which case some other steps may be necessary). Do not be a slave to your fears and attachments. Pain creates conscience; do not be afraid of pain.

NXIVM HAD NOT GRANTED access to a journalist for an article for 14 years before it gave me a tightly stage-managed tour of its leadership and operations this winter, ahead of potential indictments. It remains highly secretive and exquisitely paranoid. Members not only tape-recorded my interviews with them but had a practice of extensively taping or video recording within the group, including documenting many of Raniere's statements. They have also answered some defectors, journalists and critics with lawsuits. A New Jersey-based lawyer, Peter Skolnik, who represented the author and noted cult deprogrammer Rick Ross in a 14-year suit with Nxivm, told me that he estimated their cost of the suits at $50 million.

My initial contact within Nxivm was Clare Bronfman, one of the two Bronfman daughters who are staunch supporters. To meet her, I traveled to Mexico, where Nxivm had built educational centers and where she was staying with Raniere, in an urban location I was asked not to reveal. This was a fancy neighborhood of gated homes and German cars and builders' cranes creating more expensive apartments. They were staying there on the advice of lawyers and consultants and also because Bronfman was fearful in the United States. She was fearful here in Mexico, too, worried that someone connected with a disgruntled ex-member or someone who had read about her wealth might kidnap her when she was out for a jog.

Bronfman was wry and slight, polite. We met at one of Nxivm's midcentury-chic Mexican centers, behind a gate. She walked its airy halls, gesturing to the room where they keep their instructional materials (with a keypad lock on the door), a framed photograph of Raniere hanging on one wall and a stenciled quote from him on another — "If in the next moment your behavior would affect all of humanity for forever more, how would you behave? Every moment is such a moment."

She took a seat on a cozy couch, set up for intimate chats among members. Bronfman told me she was an introvert, and her voice was so soft that it drifted away, but she answered my questions directly and seemed highly in touch with her emotions. The only jewelry she wore was one of Tiffany's most famous pieces: a silver outline of a heart, dangling on a delicate necklace chain. She told me that she had shared a handful of necklaces with the women in the group when they were on vacation on an island she owns in Fiji, just months before Cafritz, a bubbly woman who was Raniere's most important long-term girlfriend and a beloved mother figure to Nxivm members, died from cancer. Bronfman began crying as she told me about her friend's death.

Bronfman outlined the shape of the group for me. Raniere was called "Vanguard" because he was the leader of their philosophical movement. Salzman, his first student, was "Prefect." Bronfman and everyone else were students of Vanguard's. Centers like this one were the place for Nxivm courses, though they weren't taught by Raniere, who had "duplicated" himself when he made Salzman headmistress. Nor were they often taught by Salzman anymore, but rather by members she had instructed, members whom those members had instructed, and so on. All were told not to deviate from Raniere's blueprints.

Nearby, a number of colorful sashes hung on hooks. Each color in the hierarchy was not only a higher state of self-awareness but also reflected a member's ability to recruit more members. Some higher-ranked sashes have never been attained, Bronfman whispered. You don't trade up directly to a new color of sash but first must get four silk stripes ironed onto your existing sash, a process known as "moving up the stripe path." The rigid hierarchy and doctrinaire teachings pushed members to revere those with a higher level of sash, to whom they were encouraged to pay tribute in words and deeds.

Anything in the group about skinniness, about punishment, about self-denial was simply to help members evolve. "If something's uncomfortable for us emotionally, we choose to smoke, we choose to drink, we choose to eat, we choose to dissociate," Bronfman told me. "We have so many strategies." The purpose of Nxivm was to "feel those things so that you can work them through and then they're not uncomfortable anymore."

I thought I was meeting Bronfman before I met Raniere because Raniere liked to sleep late. But after talking to ex-members, I learned there was a pattern within the group of not allowing people to meet Raniere before a Nxivm member, usually a woman, had spoken of his great gifts. Raniere, whom members have compared to Nelson Mandela and Archbishop Desmond Tutu, didn't step from behind the curtain until he had been properly introduced.

Bronfman and I had lunch together at a local restaurant, though she didn't eat because she didn't like the vegetarian options. Then we arrived at a nondescript condo building. Pushing open a heavy wood door, I was greeted by a tall woman with surging dimple creases wearing the Tiffany necklace. She wasn't authorized to speak to a journalist, so she quickly departed.

When Raniere materialized — waking from a micronap — it was as if a record skipped. He was built like a wrestler and dressed in business casual: a sky-blue polo shirt, gray slacks and round tortoise-shell glasses. He was graying at the temples, but the rest of his dark hair was cut with flair and volume. He spoke in a nasal, New York-accented voice and often tossed his hair, a feminine gesture that he used to punctuate his thoughts. He didn't seem like a man who could make other people orbit him like moons. He seemed like a high-end real estate broker trying to come off as friendly but anxious about closing a sale. "It's quite a point in life for me," he said, his eyes somewhat lost behind his glasses. "I question my values, how I conduct myself, all of these things." He later added, "I don't think I'm seen as the person I think I am, and I also want to be the person that I think I am."

Those lines portended some grand finale. And Raniere, who seemed intelligent and intensely sad, broke into tears several times, particularly when talking about Cafritz's death. He was honest about the fact that he was polyamorous and spoke to me about the importance of not only sex but intimacy. But what was important to know about him was that what he does every day is simply walk and think, he told me. He walked 14 to 20 miles a day, calculated by a Fitbit on his wrist, and during those walks, he thought about how to solve humanity's problems. "I'm like a nerd who has read too much, only I've thought too much." In Nxivm, the point of integrations was reaching what they called "unification." I asked Raniere later if he was unified. "That's more a theoretical or goal state," he told me, adding, perhaps coyly, "I don't think if someone was unified they would particularly talk about it."

Yet through many hours of conversation, Raniere did not progress to new points. There were some light spots, like when he told me that humanity needed to develop more humanity, and we deserved to, because we were a special species; cats don't have "catmanity," he said. But I watched as he drew into himself, seemingly intentionally, becoming a black hole of anti-charisma. In a slow, calm, metronomic voice, he emitted sentences about scientific and philosophical theories: whether humans are biological robots or have free will; whether mysticism is inherently bad or "a tool of understanding but is often abused"; how to interpret Zeno's dichotomy paradox, a classic logic problem; the possibility that interrelationships with families and friends persist in the afterlife.

Raniere has considered himself special for a long time: He has said he spoke in full sentences at a year old, read by 2 and taught himself to play concert-level piano at 12, the same year he learned high school math in 19 hours. His home life was something quite different, and he claimed this was what had led him to create Nxivm. His mother had a heart condition and was often in bed. She and his father fought. About the rancor, he said, "I didn't blame myself for causing it, but I didn't know why I couldn't stop it." His parents divorced when he was 8, and as an only child, he said he became his mother's "sole caregiver." She died when he was 18. Relationships outside his family became of paramount import to him.

Raniere graduated from Rensselaer Polytechnic Institute in Troy, N.Y., with a triple major in biology, mathematics and physics. He wanted to be an academic, but for a child who felt out of control, control of others may have been appealing, and he became interested in the science behind multilevel marketing. His first entrepreneurial foray was called Consumers' Buyline, which sold groceries and other goods at a discount to those who signed up for memberships. It was enormously successful, at least at first. Local papers in Albany portrayed him as an eccentric, appealing genius, noting that he slept only a few hours a night and could juggle and unicycle. Several years after its founding, Consumers' Buyline was investigated by state attorneys general as a suspected pyramid scheme, and Raniere and his associates agreed to close shop in 1997.

The structure of Consumers' Buyline brings to mind Nxivm's setup, with members recruiting other members and the way that Raniere was often introduced late in a participant's membership, standing out of reach at the top of the pyramid. It might be surprising that people would sign up for a self-improvement endeavor led by a man who might have led a pyramid scheme, but today in Nxivm, leaders explain to incoming members that Consumers' Buyline had been unfairly targeted, but Raniere refused to be vengeful and instead conceived the group as "an opposing thing that would be good in the world," as one member told me. After developing another company — a health network selling vitamins and dietary supplements and recommending alternative doctors — with his girlfriend of the time, Toni Natalie, Raniere began thinking more deeply about persuasion and how you could talk people into anything, even helping themselves.

When Raniere met Salzman, who had a successful therapy practice near Albany at the time, they began having conversations, just two people going back and forth talking, and soon, Salzman said, she started to feel better, more joyful. She asked Raniere if she could watch him do his persuasion model. "He said, 'On a person?' And I said: 'Yeah, on a person. Can I watch you do it on a person?' And he said, 'You mean other than you?'" She lowered her voice for dramatic effect. "In that moment, I went, 'Oh, my god, I do feel good.'"

LIKE RANIERE, THE BRONFMAN SISTERS were seeking to heal familial relationships, particularly with their father, a pillar of New York society and president of the World Jewish Congress. They were also drawn to Raniere's emphasis on ethics. "My whole life growing up, I always wanted to do something to impact the world," said Sara, a lovely woman who made me eggs in her Albany-area mansion this winter — the proportions of her home were so preposterous that I felt I had shrunk to a hundredth of my size, like Alice after she drank the potion in Wonderland. "My dad, as we were growing up, he was bringing Jews out of Russia, he was taking on the Swiss banks." After a friend from Sun Valley recommended the group, then called Executive Success Programs, to Sara, she asked Edgar to take a course, and he liked it. "All my dreams of saving the world with my dad were coming true," she said.

When Clare, who was a professional equestrian competitor in her early years, took her first course, she was unimpressed. Then she listened to Raniere's theory about money. Like Ayn Rand, he taught that money isn't inherently good or bad: It simply is. "I thought that money made people bad," she told me. "When I was at horse shows, I would spend time with people who didn't have money. I would never connect with people who did." But she began to realize that "money's money. And people are people. So rich people can do good and bad, poor people can do good and bad." Before Nxivm, Clare didn't deal with her finances. As a wealthy woman, it was all done for her. "My family had lawyers. My family had accountants."

A profound rift developed between Edgar and his daughters a few years into their involvement in Nxivm, but Clare continued to want to use her inherited money ethically. Raniere, like Rand, taught that dexterous use of money — the assigning of value to various goods and services — was one of humanity's highest virtues. Raniere told me money was "noble." But after the Consumers' Buyline debacle, he was careful not to put his hands on much of it himself. In fact, Salzman owns Nxivm, and Raniere has nothing to do with it, officially. He received no salary from Nxivm, nor possessed a credit card, A.T.M. card or a car. He told me, "I don't pay taxes because I live under the poverty level." I asked him where he got his clothes, which require money to buy. He answered that they usually appeared. Pointing to the polo shirt he was wearing, he said, "until I put this on this morning, I don't think I'd worn it before, and I didn't know about it."

In 2010, documents from a lawsuit stemming from a real estate dispute claimed that many millions of the Bronfman fortune had been spent in connection with Nxivm, and Raniere had also lost nearly $66 million betting on the commodities market. (Raniere insists it was less.) When I asked Raniere about his relationship with Clare Bronfman, he said only that she's "so supportive, so pure."

With access to Bronfman funds, Nxivm engaged in all manner of legacy-creating enterprises, many demonstrating kindness and concern for others. The group invited the Dalai Lama to Albany, though he initially canceled his 2009 trip after the press drew attention to the mysterious nature of the group; several members traveled to

Dharamsala to smooth things over. They've designed a "peace pledge" for Mexicans and made a film about Raniere's ideas to solve violence in the country. They formed an a cappella group named, appropriately enough, Simply Human. They host "Vanguard Week," an annual celebration of Raniere's birthday, running triathlons and solving Rubik's Cubes. Through the year, they played volleyball, Raniere's favorite sport, usually after 9 p.m., when he preferred to play.

As the group opened centers in New York City, Vancouver and, strikingly, Mexico's big cities, including Mexico City, Monterrey and Guadalajara, it became more certain than ever about the power of the tech. The day before I met Jacqueline, Salzman introduced me to an 18-year-old high school student she was trying to help surmount Crohn's disease through Nxivm's technology. Bronfman has also produced a film about Nxivm improving the symptoms of Tourette patients, which screened at the Newport Beach Film Festival this spring. Raniere had free rein to indulge his interest in scientific experiments. He conceived a new type of school to teach children as many as eight languages at a time; each teacher speaks one language, on the theory that children pick up language more easily from a beloved caregiver. I visited one of these Mexican schools in a pretty stucco building, though school wasn't in session, so I couldn't gauge the children's octolingualism.

Nxivm members also created and operate The Knife, an active website that uses "scientific analysis" to gauge the relative honor of news outlets like this one. News was disinformation that could encourage fear, start wars and convince people of anything, but the Knife wielded its powerful tool nobly. The site and its editor in chief were featured last July on "Fox and Friends."

WOMEN FILLED MANY high ranks in the group, so it is not a surprise that one of its enterprises involved gender relationships. In 2006, Raniere created Jness, a "made-up word that we are defining as we define who we are," a female member told me. Some of its teachings seemed reasonable enough: In the beginning of the course titled Raw, men and women were encouraged to talk about their gender's genuine experience of life, and sex, and how the other sex often made them feel repressed, denigrated and ashamed. By voicing these feelings, which can be taboo to speak out loud, men supposedly developed compassion for women, and vice versa. Jness cost $5,000 for each eight-day workshop, of which there are 11.

"We were so angry at each other, both genders," Lauren Salzman, Nancy's daughter, a clever 40-year-old and perhaps the group's most persuasive junior leader, told me. "Women feel oppressed, and we have so many examples of how that's true. And the men would try to stick up for themselves and we would all attack them. ... We cut them off constantly just because we're excited and impulsive. But we didn't understand that they really felt unheard or disrespected or uncared for. Or withholding sex," she continued, "we make them work for it and they just don't understand and they feel fearful and unaccepted."

In Jness, like many of Nxivm's courses, once the unspoken had been spoken, a new theory, developed by Raniere, took root. Raniere told followers that they must accept that women and men are wired differently. Men are repressed and do not enjoy the same rich experience of existence as women, but they have an understanding of right and wrong; women can be disloyal, have tantrums and get away with whatever they prefer, or as Salzman puts it, "the crazier I get, the more I get." Raniere also introduced a theory about ancient men that he called "the primitive hypothesis," emphasizing that men are naturally promiscuous, and women are naturally monogamous.

In the larger Nxivm community, most thought Raniere was celibate. But the inner circle knew that he maintained multiple relationships from his home. Consenting adults can surely engage in whatever sexual relationship they prefer, including many women having segmented and siloed relationships with one man. But though Raniere told me that he policed his relationships for ethical shortcomings, the manipulation of his girlfriends, and his girlfriends' manipulation of other girlfriends, may also have been a feature of his private life.

Barbara Bouchey, Raniere's girlfriend of nine years who left Nxivm in 2009 and was a party to 14 lawsuits involving the group and its related entities, said Raniere kept his other relationships with women, some of whom she calls his "spiritual wives," secret from her at first. When he didn't see Bouchey for a few days and she wondered where he had gone, first Raniere and then high-ranked women in the group pointed to her abandonment issues as the daughter of an alcoholic father. Her issues were the problem, not Raniere. Perhaps he was absent because he was trying to teach her a great lesson about one's expectations of another being.

The two views of Raniere — the world's most ethical man running an extraordinary self-help organization; a con man who empowered women but retained ultimate power for himself — came up often in my conversation with Bouchey. She said she is not sure if Raniere is a version of Dr. Jekyll and Mr. Hyde, but he might be. But she knew him as a loving boyfriend, affectionate and as measured as when I saw him. He almost never raised his voice, showed anger or talked condescendingly in her presence. "I've seen Keith tirelessly mentoring someone over a phobia or becoming a better speaker or giving someone piano lessons, because he has those values," she said. Later in our conversation, she told me she's haunted by one question. "Did he really love me?" she said. "I honestly felt it at times. It seemed genuine, especially in the early years."

RANIERE WAS A MASTER of disorientation, of making people believe that up was down and down was up. The way he did this, it seemed, was by promoting both positive and negative endeavors at the same time. This was most evident in the group's next series of experiments.

For men, Nxivm offered a club named the Society of Protectors. Eduardo Asunsolo, a member, told me that each huddle of men would become others' support system, and if, say, you had a new house you needed to paint, they would show up with roller brushes in hand. To his philosophical theories, Raniere had introduced his followers to a concept called "collateral," or "collateralizing your word," which members understood to be "adding extra leverage to your conscience." If a man didn't "uphold" his word about running, perhaps the whole group would forgo the next morning's coffee. "If I know my buddies can't have their coffee in the morning, I'm going to run," Asunsolo explained.

Collateral took a different form when applied to women. About three years ago, some female members began approaching others on the sly, asking if they felt stuck in their personal growth and wanted to join a secret international women-only self-help group to move quicker in their personal growth. An opening line might be: "I want to talk to you about something that will change your life." But there was one odd aspect to this overture: This particular self-help scheme did not cost anything. In Raniere's Randian utopia, true value exchange was always upheld. Everyone paid for courses, or worked fees off through administrative tasks or perhaps nannying for richer members. Some went into debt.

In order to learn more about this secret society, to even get the pitch, invitees had to turn over something valuable. And what was truly valuable in life? These were mostly affluent women, so it couldn't be a diamond necklace; they could always get another. It needed to be something that, if lost, would punish you or damage you — a nude photo, a video confessional about a law you'd broken, maybe even the deed to your house, signed over. This was true collateral, the most direct way to show your trust. And only through complete trust could you truly love another person. You might also call it blackmail.

Michele, a 31-year-old member, told me about her experience of joining this group, which some women called the Vow, and others referred to by the solemn name Dominus Obsequious Sororium, broken Latin for "lord over the obedient female companions," or DOS for short. (Raniere described it to me as a "sorority.") One day in Albany, Michele recalled that a member asked her to lunch. "This was someone I really admired from afar. I was superexcited and flattered that she wanted to talk to me." She told me, "I knew if she was involved, there were probably other badass women involved, and I want to be a badass woman — I'm struggling to do that." Michele said she found her experience of giving collateral "growthful."

To this day, dedicated DOS members insist that they began the secret group themselves when one of them was deeply upset and others decided to help her by pledging ultimate commitment. Over time, the group morphed into a military-style boot camp that was simply trying to address the place of women in the world, to make them realize that they were not victims.

When I visited Mack in her gorgeous apartment in Brooklyn — paintings by an ex-boyfriend resting against a wall, Palo Santo just burned in an incense dish — she told me this, too. With a bright smile, Mack, who came to Nxivm when she was unhappy with her TV acting career (she asked Raniere to "make her a great actress again"), explained the way DOS worked. She gestured to a beige love seat and asked if I wanted to sit down, near the tape recorders.

The woman who invited you to the group was your master, Mack said, tucking her blue-socked feet under her, or the "representation of your conscience, your higher self, your most ideal." Masters would help slaves count calories to save them from the trap of emotional eating, according to other women in the group. Masters would dictate an act of "self-denial," like cold showers or rousing yourself from bed at 4 a.m. and standing stock still for a time. Slaves were told to do "acts of care" for masters, perhaps bringing them coffee. Slaves might be told to abstain from orgasms, ostensibly to heal their negative sexual patterns. Mack said that this was "about devotion" and "like any spiritual practice or religion." I thought about free will — did she believe in that? She said, "You're dedicating your life one way or another."

Mack recruited other women and even tweeted at famous women like Emma Watson, inviting them to learn more about her techniques of female empowerment. Many women told me they improved from this scheme, and Mack agreed. "I found my spine, and I just kept solidifying my spine every time I would do something hard," Mack said passionately. DOS was "about women coming together and pledging to one another a full-time commitment to become our most powerful and embodied selves by pushing on our greatest fears, by exposing our greatest vulnerabilities, by knowing that we would stand with each other no matter what, by holding our word, by overcoming pain."

When the cauterized brand was introduced, it was a scary experience, like any real rite of passage, but some of them kidded around through it. Even if they cried when they were getting the brand; even if they wore surgical masks to help them with breathing in the smell of burning flesh; even if the brand was much larger than they were told it would be and looked like an ancient hieroglyph; even if they were in a state of sheer terror, they were still able to transcend the fear and cry out to one another: "Badass warrior bitches! Let's get strong together."

In yet another pyramid of the scheme, each master was supposed to bring in slaves, and then, to become masters, those slaves would recruit slaves of their own; an estimated 150 women ultimately joined. Some slaves called each other "sisters." Mack told me each circle was "like a little family."

Though a majority of women in DOS never had anything to do with Raniere sexually (to me, he was only willing to admit to two) and thus it is impossible to say that DOS itself was a "sex-slave cult" rather than a sex-slave cult and a women's empowerment scheme, most of the women had been indoctrinated into Jness's ideas and thus believed that men were inclined toward polyamory and women not, and that in Clifton Park, the natural order of the genders was being taught. Promising to seduce Raniere — which was apparently the way he preferred to be approached sexually, rather than putting himself on the line — was also one of the ways some women later said they were told to show commitment to the sisterhood. It was a test of faith in DOS, a proof of ultimate commitment, of loyalty. And if you didn't have faith, DOS wouldn't work for you, and you would lose all your sisters and your chance at badassness.

In her apartment, I was surprised to hear Mack take full responsibility for coming up with the DOS cauterized brand. She told me, "I was like: 'Y'all, a tattoo? People get drunk and tattooed on their ankle 'BFF,' or a tramp stamp. I have two tattoos and they mean nothing.'" She wanted to do something more meaningful, something that took guts.

To be honest, I was surprised that she was sitting there at all. And Mack told me that she'd been experiencing some anxiety talking to a reporter. It felt "scary and pressureful," she said. But Lauren Salzman, who along with Raniere and Clare Bronfman had guided my highly controlled tour of their world, helped her by telling Mack to cast her mind back to when she was a child and received praise at the same time that other kids didn't. This made Mack feel uncomfortable. But now she was surmounting her fear. "So when I was 8, I created a conclusion and built a foundation of my assumptions that was faulty," she told me. "Now that I'm 35, I can look back at that 8-year-old's belief. And I can say, 'Oh, that doesn't make any sense anymore.'" She continued, "Boom, my belief system is upgraded."

BELIEF IS A TRICKY THING, particularly when it involves taking responsibility for the idea of branding women and being encouraged to talk to a journalist when it may not be in your self-interest to do so. All the more when you include a guru who is an "evolved" being, Explorations of Meaning, "integrations," joy, hierarchy, money, the stripe path, extreme dieting, secret polyamory and outward-facing benevolent ventures. By the point that many women signed up for DOS, they had taken many steps where they felt they had given consent.

While the concept of collateral might have been growthful for Michele, others describe it as a horrifying experience, particularly when they were told to submit additional pieces of collateral sharing the deepest secrets of their parents or those close to them. They felt there was no way out, that their real family wouldn't accept them after this betrayal. Even today, the overall shame of being identified not only as a member of a cult but as a "sex slave" — of having their control and choice, and, essentially, humanity, stripped from them — has kept many silent.

After I interviewed him in Mexico, Raniere stopped using a phone and used an untraceable email account. He relocated to a villa in Puerto Vallarta, which is where he was found by the Mexican authorities this spring in the company of Mack and other women. As he was driven away from the villa in a police car, according to prosecutors, the women gave chase. They were not ready to give up their guru yet. If they let him leave, perhaps they would be exhibiting weakness or hitting against an emotional problem that needed attention.

Friday, April 13, was the date set for Raniere's arraignment in a New York federal court. Within a week, Mack was arrested on the same charges as Raniere. The F.B.I. accused Raniere of "a disgusting abuse of power in his efforts to denigrate and manipulate women he considered his sex slaves ... within this unorthodox pyramid scheme." The criminal complaint claimed that the severe DOS diet was not for the women's good, but to please Raniere, who, it asserted, sexually prefers very thin women, whom he entertained in a Clifton Park bachelor pad called "the Library," outfitted with a bed and a hot tub. Prosecutors also claimed that Raniere, in the 1980s and early 1990s, had repeated sexual encounters with under-age girls. (He denied this to me.)

Mack was Raniere's personal slave, according to the F.B.I. The collateral she gave him as her "master" was chilling: a contract declaring that if she broke her commitment, her home would be transferred into his name and future children birthed by her would be his, as well as a letter addressed to social services claiming abuse of her nephews. And when slaves took nude photos and gave them to masters as "collateral," believing only women were involved in the group, Mack sent some collateral to Raniere. In one case, upon receiving digital photos, Raniere sent her a text reading "all mine?" with a smiling devil emoji.

Perhaps in order to please him, Mack decided to take on appealing young women as her slaves; she told me she knew she needed to "get right" with her longstanding jealousy issues with younger, more attractive women. Allegations include that late at night, she set up a slave on a walk with Raniere. He blindfolded the slave, led her to what seemed like a shack and tied her to a table, after which another person, whom she hadn't met before, performed oral sex on her. Mack pleaded not guilty to the charges against her, but eventually people noticed that the symbol branded on the women not only included a "KR" but also seemed to have an "AM." She may have been, then, both victim and victimizer.

IN MEXICO, RANIERE INSISTED to me that claiming he brainwashed anyone was ridiculous. Brainwashing was a farce, a scientific impossibility, and indoctrination can be positive. "What is wrongful about my indoctrination?" he asked, rhetorically. But some ex-members disagree. Raniere's ex-girlfriends from the 1990s and 2000s with whom I spoke said that while they were not expressly part of a master-slave ring, they felt entrapped by this exceedingly strange man, who was a whirling dervish of ideas, but also sort of lazy, spending his days monologuing to devotees, playing volleyball, bedding women and making women do his bidding with other women. "He's got everything exactly the way he wants it," one ex-member declared in court documents. "He's not trying to succeed; he's trying to enslave."

What they learned from Nxivm was that humans are highly programmable. Free will is a limited quantity at best. It has to be earned by intensely building self-awareness, as well as an awareness of others, and their potential for manipulating you.

Raniere did not express remorse about his claimed role in DOS nor even admit to it to me. He was a wandering prophet, not a mastermind; he talked to me about angry former lovers, ex-members' "loose lips" and extortion letters that had come his way.

When addressing allegations by ex-members of abusing his power, Raniere gave me an answer steeped in Randian principles of value exchange. "I think in many of those circumstances, I'm investing," he told me, pursing his lips a little. "And when they accuse me of taking from them, I say, 'You know, honestly, I'm investing, so if anything, maybe I don't get a return on my investment, but I made that choice.' "

Before he was arrested, Raniere reminded the remaining flock that reports about Nxivm in the media could not be trusted. The media was dishonorable. And the Nxians weren't wrong that reporters were gunning for them: While I was in Albany, a photographer in a black pickup truck drove hastily by a group of women with whom I was standing, and we could see him snapping pictures inside the cab; it felt threatening and invasive, and I could see how Bronfman and others could be worried that they could be hurt.

Raniere also stressed that departing members were under the sway of the scientific principle of cognitive dissonance. They had decided he was bad, thereby they had to make him very bad, to make their defection feel good; they would probably claim that the 18-year-old with Crohn's disease I met in Salzman's kitchen was just there for Raniere to bed her. To bolster the point that Raniere was the ethical one, he noted that DOS has not publicly released any woman's "collateral" (this isn't an impressive point, given how legally problematic that would be). But he also told me that Nxivm hasn't publicly released information about defectors' private lives, traumas and family issues, knowledge they clearly possess. He insisted that he wouldn't give up that trust.

At an early May hearing for both Raniere and Mack at United States District Court for the Eastern District of New York, in Brooklyn, Raniere's lawyer, Marc Agnifilo, whose firm represented Dominique Strauss-Kahn and is currently employed by Harvey Weinstein, told a crowd of reporters that Raniere was unwilling to plea bargain. "Everything was utterly consensual — it was adults making decisions on their own of their own free will, and that's what the trial is going to show," Agnifilo said. "A lot of adult, strong-minded, free-willed women made decisions for their own lives."

Federal sex-trafficking laws meant to protect women and girls impacted by poverty and exploited may apply to the odd nexus of possible coercive sex and forms of commerce in DOS. Each charge of sex trafficking carries a 15-year minimum sentence. New criminal charges may also include racketeering, on the theory that the DOS organization in general was devoted to criminality, as well as financial charges related to supposed crimes previously outlined by an apostate girlfriend, such as bringing cash from Nxivm classes taught in Mexico over the border and visa violations.

In the hushed, carpeted courtroom, a judge sat on the terribly tall bench as three female prosecutors in sharp stiletto heels faced Raniere, and Moira Kim Penza, the lead prosecutor, wove an argument about her case.

Raniere and Mack did not look at each other once. Raniere wore a gray jumpsuit, wrinkled in the back from perhaps lying down in his cell; when he entered, his eyes darted to and fro. Mack's hair had lost its blond highlights, and she was painfully skinny. She held herself completely still except for a tiny shake.

VANESSA GRIGORIADIS is a contributing writer for The New York Times Magazine. Her book about consent and sexual assault on campus, "Blurred Lines," was published in 2017.

Glossary

adherent A person who believes in and supports a particular person or set of ideas.

allegation A claim, usually without evidence, that someone has done something wrong or illegal.

arraignment The appearance of a criminal defendant before a judge during which the charge is read and to which the defendant must plead guilty or not guilty.

ascension The rising of a person to heaven.

astrology The study of the positions and movements of the sun, moon, planets and stars in the belief that they affect the lives and character of human beings.

brand To burn an identifying mark on a living being.

cauterize To burn the skin with a hot instrument; typically used to stop bleeding.

charlatan A person who falsely claims to have special knowledge, skills or powers.

compound An enclosed group of buildings for use by people with a shared purpose.

cult A group with socially deviant or unusual, often religious, beliefs or practices.

epitomize To be a perfect example of something.

establishment Used by the counterculture in the 1960s to mean conventional social, political and economic principles of a society to which they stood in opposition.

extradition The surrendering of an alleged criminal by one country to another for the purposes of trying the charge.

extraterrestrial Anything that is of or from outside the earth or its atmosphere.

free love The practice of having sexual relations according to choice without restrictions of marriage or other long-term relationships.

grand jury A group of 23 citizens who examine accusations against a person charged with a crime and determine whether the evidence justifies proceeding with formal charges.

guru A spiritual teacher.

hedonism The belief and practice that pleasure is the most important thing in life.

hyperbole Exaggerated statements.

insatiable An appetite that is impossible to satisfy.

megalomaniac A person who is obsessed with his or her own power.

nomadic Moving from place to place.

reincarnation The belief that when a person's body dies his or her soul is reborn in another body.

sect A group that has separated from an established religion.

spurious False.

testify To make a statement under oath in court.

warrant A legal document authorizing the arrest of a person.

zealot A person who has extremely strong religious, political or philosophical ideas and tries to convince others to believe them.

Media Literacy Terms

"Media literacy" refers to the ability to access, understand, critically assess and create media. The following terms are important components of media literacy, and they will help you critically engage with the articles in this title.

angle The aspect of a news story on which a journalist focuses and develops.

attribution The method by which a source is identified or by which facts and information are assigned to the person who provided them.

balance Principle of journalism that both perspectives of an argument should be presented in a fair way.

chronological order Method of writing a story presenting the details of the story in the order in which they occurred.

commentary Type of story that is an expression of opinion on recent events by a journalist generally known as a commentator.

credibility The quality of being trustworthy and believable, said of a journalistic source.

critical review Type of story that describes an event or work of art, such as a theater performance, film, concert, book, restaurant, radio or television program, exhibition or musical piece, and offers critical assessment of its quality and reception.

editorial Article of opinion or interpretation.

feature story Article designed to entertain as well as to inform.

headline Type, usually 18 point or larger, used to introduce a story.

human interest story Type of story that focuses on individuals and how events or issues affect their lives, generally offering a sense of relatability to the reader.

impartiality Principle of journalism that a story should not reflect a journalist's bias and should contain balance.

intention The motive or reason behind something, such as the publication of a news story.

interview story Type of story in which the facts are gathered primarily by interviewing another person or persons.

motive The reason behind something, such as the publication of a news story or a source's perspective on an issue.

news story An article or style of expository writing that reports news, generally in a straightforward fashion and without editorial comment.

op-ed An opinion piece that reflects a prominent individual's opinion on a topic of interest.

paraphrase The summary of an individual's words, with attribution, rather than a direct quotation of their exact words.

quotation The use of an individual's exact words indicated by the use of quotation marks and proper attribution.

reliability The quality of being dependable and accurate, said of a journalistic source.

rhetorical device Technique in writing intending to persuade the reader or communicate a message from a certain perspective.

source The origin of the information reported in journalism.

style A distinctive use of language in writing or speech; also a news or publishing organization's rules for consistent use of language with regards to spelling, punctuation, typography and capitalization, usually regimented by a house style guide.

tone A manner of expression in writing or speech.

Media Literacy Questions

1. What is the intention of the article "Charlie Manson, Nomadic Guru, Flirted with Crime in a Turbulent Childhood" (on page 16)? How effectively does the journalist achieve this purpose?

2. Does Alex Williams demonstrate the journalistic principle of impartiality in the article "How Charles Manson Nearly Made It in Hollywood" (on page 31)? If so, how? If not, how could he have made the article more impartial?

3. "Charles Manson Dies at 83; Wild-Eyed Leader of a Murderous Crew" (on page 37) features photographs of Charles Manson, members of the Manson family and some of their victims. What do these photographs add to the article?

4. What type of story is "Pastor a Charlatan to Some, a Philosopher to Wife" (on page 56)? Can you identify another article in this collection that is the same type of story? What elements help you come to your conclusion?

5. What is the intention of the article "Cult Chief's Beginnings in Indianapolis Recalled" (on page 76)? How effectively does it achieve its intended purpose?

6. Compare the headlines of "Talks With Leader of Sect Have Stalled" (on page 117) and "Koresh, on Tape, Screams About Children" (on page 134). Which is a more compelling headline, and why?

How could the less compelling headline be changed to better draw the reader's interest?

7. "Manacles of the Mind" (on page 131) is an example of an op-ed. Identify how Jan Jarboe's attitude and tone help convey her opinion on the topic.

8. Identify each of the sources in "Leader Believed in Space Aliens and Apocalypse" (on page 137) as a primary or a secondary source. Evaluate the reliability and credibility of each source. How does your evaluation of each source change your perspective on the article?

9. In "Families Learning of 39 Cultists Who Died Willingly" (on page 143), B. Drummond Ayres Jr. directly quotes Heaven's Gate cult members and investigators. What are the strengths of the use of a direct quote as opposed to a paraphrase? What are the weaknesses?

10. Analyze the authors' reporting in "Heaven's Gate Fit in With New Mexico's Offbeat Style" (on page 157) and "Former Cultists Warn of Believers Now Adrift" (on page 161). Do you think one journalist is more balanced in his reporting than the other? If so, why do you think so?

11. Does "Authorities Raid Homes Linked to Cultlike Group That Branded Women" (on page 185) use multiple sources? What are the strengths of using multiple sources in a journalistic piece? What are the weaknesses of relying heavily on only one or a few sources?

12. "Inside Nxivm, the 'Sex Cult' That Preached Empowerment" (on page 187) is an example of an interview. What are the benefits of providing readers with direct quotes of an interviewed subject's speech? Is the subject of an interview always a reliable source?

Citations

All citations in this list are formatted according to the Modern Language Association's (MLA) style guide.

BOOK CITATION

THE NEW YORK TIMES EDITORIAL STAFF. *Cult Leaders: Charles Manson, Jim Jones and Others.* New York: New York Times Educational Publishing, 2020.

ONLINE ARTICLE CITATIONS

APPLEBOME, PETER. "Bloody Sunday's Roots in Deep Religious Soil." *The New York Times*, 2 Mar. 1993, https://www.nytimes.com/1993/03/02/us/shootout-in-texas-bloody-sunday-s-roots-in-deep-religious-soil.html.

APPLEBOME, PETER. "Talks With Leader of Sect Have Stalled." *The New York Times*, 8 Mar. 1993, https://www.nytimes.com/1993/03/08/us/talks-with-leader-of-sect-have-stalled.html.

AYRES, B. DRUMMOND, JR. "Families Learning of 39 Cultists Who Died Willingly," *The New York Times*, 29 Mar. 1997, https://www.nytimes.com/1997/03/29/us/families-learning-of-39-cultists-who-died-willingly.html.

BROOKE, JAMES. "Former Cultists Warn of Believers Now Adrift." *The New York Times*, 2 Apr. 1997, https://www.nytimes.com/1997/04/02/us/former-cultists-warn-of-believers-now-adrift.html.

BRUNI, FRANK. "Leader Believed in Space Aliens and Apocalypse." *The New York Times*, 28 Mar. 1997, https://www.nytimes.com/1997/03/28/us/leader-believed-in-space-aliens-and-apocalypse.html.

FERON, JAMES. "Cult Chief's Beginnings in Indianapolis Recalled." *The New York Times*, 22 Nov. 1977, https://www.nytimes.com/1978/11/22/archives/cult-chiefs-beginnings-in-indianapolis-recalled-cosmic-proportions.html.

FOSBURGH, LACEY. "Jones Used Bible-Thumping and Politics of Brotherhood." *The New York Times*, 22 Nov. 1977, https://www.nytimes.com/1978/11/23/archives/jones-used-biblethumping-and-politics-of-brotherhood-mixture-of.html.

FOX, MARGALIT. "Charles Manson Dies at 83; Wild-Eyed Leader of a Murderous Crew." *The New York Times*, 20 Nov. 2017, https://www.nytimes.com/2017/11/20/obituaries/charles-manson-dead.html.

GOLDBERG, CAREY. "Heaven's Gate Fit in With New Mexico's Offbeat Style." *The New York Times*, 31 Mar. 1997, https://www.nytimes.com/1997/03/31/us/heaven-s-gate-fit-in-with-new-mexico-s-offbeat-style.html.

GRIGORIADIS, VANESSA. "Inside Nxivm, the 'Sex Cult' That Preached Empowerment." *The New York Times*, 30 May 2018, https://www.nytimes.com/2018/05/30/magazine/sex-cult-empowerment-nxivm-keith-raniere.html.

HAAG, MATTHEW. "Charles Manson's Remains Will Go to Purported Grandson, Judge Rules." *The New York Times*, 12 Mar. 2018, https://www.nytimes.com/2018/03/12/us/charles-manson-body-grandson.html.

JARBOE, JAN. "Manacles of the Mind." *The New York Times*, 21 Apr. 1993, https://www.nytimes.com/1993/04/21/opinion/manacles-of-the-mind.html.

JOHNSTON, DAVID. "Koresh, on Tape, Screams About Children." *The New York Times*, 10 June 1993, https://www.nytimes.com/1993/06/10/us/koresh-on-tape-screams-about-children.html.

LINDSEY, ROBERT. "Defectors From Sect Depict Its Rehearsals for Suicide." *The New York Times*, 21 Nov. 1977, https://www.nytimes.com/1978/11/21/archives/defectors-from-sect-depict-its-rehearsals-for-suicide-defectors-say.html.

LINDSEY, ROBERT. "Jim Jones — From Poverty to Power of Life and Death." *The New York Times*, 21 Nov. 1977, https://www.nytimes.com/1978/11/26/archives/jim-jonesfrom-poverty-to-power-of-life-and-death-arrested-for-lewd.html.

MEIER, BARRY. "Authorities Raid Homes Linked to Cultlike Group That Branded Women." *The New York Times*, 27 Mar. 2018, https://www.nytimes.com/2018/03/27/nyregion/nxivm-leader-raids.html.

MEIER, BARRY. "Charges Filed Against Leader of Secretive Group Where Women Were Branded." *The New York Times*, 26 Mar. 2018, https://www.nytimes.com/2018/03/26/nyregion/keith-raniere-arrested-nxivm.html.

MEIER, BARRY. "Inside a Secretive Group Where Women Are Branded." *The New York Times*, 17 Oct. 2017, https://www.nytimes.com/2017/10/17/nyregion/nxivm-women-branded-albany.html.

MEIER, BARRY, AND PAULINA VILLEGAS. "Federal Officials Reportedly Investigating Group Where Women Were Branded." *The New York Times*, 21 Dec. 2017, https://www.nytimes.com/2017/12/21/nyregion/nxivm-women-branded-federal-investigation.html.

MILLOY, ROSS E. "Death in Waco: A Fiery End; An Angry Telephone Call

Signals the End of the World for Cult Members." *The New York Times*, 20 Apr. 1993, https://www.nytimes.com/1993/04/20/us/death-waco-fiery-end-angry-telephone-call-signals-end-world-for-cult-members.html.

THE NEW YORK TIMES. "Cult Leader Gives 'Letter From God'." *The New York Times*, 11 Apr. 1993, https://www.nytimes.com/1993/04/11/us/cult-leader-gives-letter-from-god.html.

THE NEW YORK TIMES. "Gateway to Madness." *The New York Times*, 29 Mar. 1997, https://www.nytimes.com/1997/03/29/opinion/gateway-to-madness.html.

THE NEW YORK TIMES. "Jones and 3 in Family Are to Be Buried at Sea." *The New York Times*, 27 Nov. 1977, https://www.nytimes.com/1978/11/27/archives/jones-and-3-in-family-are-to-be-buried-at-sea.html.

THE NEW YORK TIMES. "Letters to the Editor." *The New York Times*, 5 Apr. 1997, https://www.nytimes.com/1997/04/05/opinion/l-cultists-tragedy-defies-our-understanding-468150.html.

THE NEW YORK TIMES. "Suicide Cult's Possessions Auctioned Off." *The New York Times*, 22 Nov. 1999, https://www.nytimes.com/1999/11/22/us/suicide-cult-s-possessions-auctioned-off.html.

NORDHEIMER, JON. "Leader of Sect Dies." *The New York Times*, 26 Nov. 1977, https://www.nytimes.com/1978/11/21/archives/leader-of-sect-dies-parents-reported-to-give-children-poison-before.html.

NOSSITER, ADAM. "Warning of Violence Was Unheeded After Cult Leader's Gun Battle in '87." *The New York Times*, 10 Mar. 1993, https://www.nytimes.com/1993/03/10/us/warning-of-violence-was-unheeded-after-cult-leader-s-gun-battle-in-87.html.

PADNANI, AMISHA. "What Became of the Manson Family?" *The New York Times*, 20 Nov. 2017, https://www.nytimes.com/2017/11/20/us/what-ever-happened-to-the-manson-family.html.

PURDUM, TODD S. "In Serene Setting in California, a Suicide Investigation Unfolds." *The New York Times*, 30 Mar. 1997, https://www.nytimes.com/1997/03/30/us/in-serene-setting-in-california-a-suicide-investigation-unfolds.html.

ROBERTS, STEVEN V. "Charlie Manson, Nomadic Guru, Flirted With Crime in a Turbulent Childhood." *The New York Times*, 7 Dec. 1969, https://timesmachine.nytimes.com/timesmachine/1969/12/07/89389219.html.

ROBERTS, STEVEN V. "Head of the 'Family' Is Held For Trial." *The New York Times*, 4 Dec. 1969, https://timesmachine.nytimes.com/timesmachine/1969

/12/04/88868478.html.

ROBERTS, STEVEN V. “Manson Case: People Keep Asking — ‘What Made Those Kids Do It?’” *The New York Times*, 31 Jan. 1971, https://timesmachine.nytimes.com/timesmachine/1971/01/31/81872240.html.

ROBERTS, STEVEN V. “Manson: The Two Faces of a Man on Trial.” *The New York Times*, 3 Jan. 1971, https://timesmachine.nytimes.com/timesmachine/1971/01/03/91261044.html.

ROBERTS, STEVEN V. “3 Suspects in Tate Case Tied to Guru and ‘Family’.” *The New York Times*, 3 Dec. 1969, https://timesmachine.nytimes.com/timesmachine/1969/12/03/91292891.html.

ROBINSON, DOUGLAS. “Manson Called a Megalomaniac by Prosecutor as Trial Begins.” *The New York Times*, 25 July 1970, https://www.nytimes.com/1970/07/25/archives/manson-called-a-megalomaniac-by-prosecutor-as-trial-begins.html.

TURNER, WALLACE. “Deaths in Guyana Threaten Sect’s California Organization.” *The New York Times*, 20 Nov. 1978, https://www.nytimes.com/1978/11/20/archives/deaths-in-guyana-threaten-sects-california-organization-jones-is.html.

TURNER, WALLACE. “Dispute Over Baby Spurred Sect’s Move to Guyana.” *The New York Times*, 19 Nov. 1978, https://www.nytimes.com/1978/11/19/archives/dispute-over-baby-spurred-sects-move-to-guyana-chairman-of-housing.html.

TURNER, WALLACE. “Pastor a Charlatan to Some, a Philosopher to Wife.” *The New York Times*, 2 Sept. 1977, https://www.nytimes.com/1977/09/02/archives/pastor-a-charlatan-to-some-a-philosopher-to-wife.html.

VERHOVEK, SAM HOWE. “ ‘Messiah’ Fond of Bible, Rock and Women.” *The New York Times*, 3 Mar. 1993, https://www.nytimes.com/1993/03/03/us/messiah-fond-of-bible-rock-and-women.html.

VERHOVEK, SAM HOWE. “With Plenty of Food, Water and Bibles, Texas Cult Can Hold Out for a While.” *The New York Times*, 5 Mar. 1993, https://www.nytimes.com/1993/03/05/us/with-plenty-of-food-water-and-bibles-texas-cult-can-hold-out-for-a-while.html.

WILLIAMS, ALEX. “How Charles Manson Nearly Made It in Hollywood.” *The New York Times*, 21 Nov. 2017, https://www.nytimes.com/2017/11/21/style/charles-manson-annoying-hipster.html.

Index

This book is current up until the time of printing. For the most up-to-date reporting, visit www.nytimes.com.